You Broke my heart

was it love?

By

Kanishk Chourasia

i

RIGI PUBLICATION

YOU BROKE MY HEART
WAS IT LOVE ?

By

Kanishk Chourasia

Originally published in India
ISBN: 978-93-84314-43-9

Published by RIGI PUBLICATION
777, Street no.9, Krishna Nagar
Khanna-141401 (Punjab), India
Website: www.rigipublication.com
Email: info@rigipublication.com
Phone: +91-9357710014, +91-9465468291

INDEX

A Call

It was Friday afternoon and I was working in the office while talking to my colleague about the ongoing project and thinking about going for lunch. Generally, we used to go to lunch around 12.30 to 1 o'clock as the canteen gets crowded and we won't get enough space to sit around.

Meanwhile, I got a call from an unknown number and due to network problem I came out from ODC (offshore development center) to receive the call.

"Hello, who's this?"

A soothing voice from the other end answered. "Is this Harsh speaking?"

"Yes, speaking" I replied.

"Do you know Ajay?" She asked.

"Yes, he is my friend, what happened? Is it anything serious?" I enquired.

"Your friend met with an accident and he is in serious condition. Can you quickly come down to City hospital, Pune?" She replied.

I was in a state of shock after hearing this.

"I am coming as soon as possible." I said and disconnected.

I was totally blank for a moment and was not able to decide what to do and whom to call. Then I called up our common friends and informed them about the accident and asked them to come down to city hospital as soon as possible.

After that I came inside the ODC, where I was working. As I was in a state of shock, so my colleague asked me about the call and if anything was serious.

I told him that a close friend of mine met with an accident and he is in serious condition so I have to leave immediately for the City hospital where he has been admitted. I requested him to inform our manager about the situation.

"Call me if anything is urgent, else we can discuss it on Monday. Bye for now." I said and I left the office.

"Don't worry, I will handle this, leave as of now and drive safely and call me if possible once you reach there." Sagar (my colleague) said.

Our office was located on the fifth floor and it was 1o'clock towards the evening as of now and lunch time had begun so I took my bag and began strolling towards the way out. Everybody around inquired as to whether all was well as I was leaving early. I informed them about the state of my friend and left from that point.

I reached the elevator, but it was on the ground floor and it was taking a lot of time. So I took stairs as I was in a hurry. After reaching the parking zone I took my vehicle and started driving towards the hospital, it was close to 10 km from my office and it was quite hot in the afternoon.

After reaching the hospital parking lot, I called back on the same number and said that I have reached. I asked "Can you help me with the details of my friend, the ward and all?"

She asked me to come directly to the first floor and from there she would take me to where he was admitted. I reached the first floor and again called her as soon as she received the call and she started speaking; I realized she was standing in front of me.

"Hi, this is Harsh" I went near and asked her. "Are you the same person who called me earlier to tell me about my friend's accident?"

"Yes," she said "I am Archana, I called up to inform you about your friend's accident, presently he is in the operation theatre so you can't meet him."

I asked her if everything is fine or is it a matter of concern.

She asked me to wait patiently until his operation.

I asked her if she had informed his parents about the accident.

She told me that his phone was severely damaged and she could not retrieve any other number and that she fortunately found my number written in a small diary inside his wallet so she called me up. She also asked me to inform his parents if I have their number. But I do not have their number.

Soon I received a call from Karan, a common friend. He asked me where I am, as he was in the hospital's parking zone.

"I am on the first floor." I said and asked him to come there.

After he reached the first floor I saw he was panicked. He showered me with multiple questions…How is Ajay? Where is he? Is everything okay?

I told him about Ajay being operated and that we need to wait. I also told him that we needed to inform his parents.

As we sat waiting outside the operation theatre, Karan asked me how all this happened? I told him that I am unaware about how it happened. Do you have Ajay's parents' number? He said," I don't have their number probably Uzair might be having, I will check with him."

Almost an hour has passed by, we were very tense and nervous and in between Karan called Uzair and asked for Ajay's parents' number. After that Karan asked me to talk to his parents as he was in a panic and was unable to talk. I too was in a dilemma as to how to inform Ajay's parents about this. But I took a deep breath, gathered some strength and then started dialing Ajay's father's number, as the phone was ringing my heartbeat raced.

In between Ajay's father received the call and said "Hello, Who's this?" I was stammering and I said "hi hello hello, this is Harsh, Ajay's friend."

I told him that Ajay has met with an accident and he has been admitted to City hospital and asked him to come there. I also told him that Karan and I are here and he need not worry much.

It was 3 o'clock in the afternoon and we both were sitting patiently when suddenly the door of the OT (operation theatre) opened and we looked attentively to the door and wishing everything is fine, we moved towards the door curiously.

We saw Dr. Archana coming out of the operation theater so we went near her and before we could ask her "How is Ajay?" She said, "Everything is fine." Only we know how comforting those three words were. We asked her if we could meet him. To which she replied "he is unconscious at the moment, so you can't meet him now" and she walked off.

We saw one family coming towards us. I recognized their faces, as once Ajay has shown his family photograph. So, I went near his father and said "Hello uncle, I am Harsh, I called you."

I saw Ajay's father was very tense and nervous and his mother was crying.

He asked me "Is everything okay? Where is my son?"

"Dr. Archana just informed me that everything is fine and we need not worry" I said and when I looked at his mother she was still crying so I said, "Please stop crying aunty, everything is fine so you need not worry."

But I know a mother's heart, she is the person who has given birth to him and who was very dear to her, so it was extremely difficult for her to control her emotions, but they say a mother is a mother, and we being friends were hurt at the core, our hearts sobbed as well.

After that I went to the reception to inform them that Ajay's family is here, and now they can talk to Ajay's father.

Soon Dr. Archana arrived, I introduced her to Ajay's father, after which she took Ajay's father along with her to talk something personal… Aunty was still crying in spite of convincing her so much she was not willing to listen.

It was 5 o'clock in the evening; Dr. Archana came and said "you can meet Ajay."

We went inside to see Ajay and we saw that his leg was fractured and even his head had injuries. He has received multiple injuries so we knew that his state was not very good and it was something very serious. Looking at this Ajay's mother burst out in tears and at this I couldn't control myself and I came out of the operation theatre and started crying alone. Karan was in a dilemma as to whom to console first.

Meanwhile, Dr. Archana came and told us to come out of the operation theatre as some other procedures were pending.

We all were very upset and were waiting for Ajay to come back to his senses. As the time passed by we looked at the watch and hoped to talk to Ajay soon. I and Karan came down to parking zone and meanwhile I called my brother "I may not be able to come home as my friend has met with an accident and is in very serious condition. So I will stay back at the hospital"

"Do I need to come there?" my brother asked.

"No, if required I will let you know." I said and disconnected.

We were really very hungry, so came out of the hospital premises and headed to a juice centre across the road. We quenched ourselves and also took a parcel for them. After coming upstairs we offered the juice to his parents but aunty was hesitating and we tried hard to convince her as she hadn't eaten anything since morning. "Thank God" at last she took.

It was around 8 o'clock and we were still waiting in the lobby when a nurse came and said "Ajay has gained consciousness, so you all can meet him now." We all hurriedly went inside to have a glimpse of Ajay. After seeing him we feel relaxed. We tried to talk to him, but he was not able to talk as the doctor has advised him to have ample rest.

Ajay's father asked us to go home since we had been there since afternoon, but we refused to go since we too wanted to stay back. Finally, we convinced uncle that we would be staying back, so at last he agreed.

After that we went into the dormitory as we all were sitting together, I told Karan to bring something to eat since we all were really hungry. Also, I told him to get juice for Ajay.

Karan came back with the parcel, we all had dinner together and then Karan and I came down to have a stroll...as we walked we were having a chat about Ajay and Aastha.

Oh!, I forgot... Who is Aastha? By the way she is Ajay's girlfriend.

In between uncle called me to come back upstairs urgently as he had forgotten the medicine pattern which the doctor has prescribed to Ajay. We both went upstairs and I told uncle which medicine is to be given to Ajay, since we both were only there at the time when the doctor was explaining.

It was around 11o'clock and we all were very tired and feeling sleepy so Karan and I along with uncle came outside to sleep but aunty was sitting beside Ajay on his bed. We slept and didn't realize we were so tired that we could doze off so quickly. When we woke up it was 6 o'clock in the morning.

I saw uncle and aunty were already awake and were beside Ajay. I told uncle that I will go home and come back with breakfast since my home was nearby hospital. Once I came back from home with the breakfast we all had it together after that uncle and aunty went down and Karan and I stayed back with Ajay.

I asked Ajay how he felt.

"I am feeling much better. Thanks for being here." He said.

I asked him "How this all happened?"

He replied that he was going to the office, but all the time he was thinking about her (Aastha) and suddenly there was a signal which he didn't realize and he was driving at very high speed. He jumped the signal and a car from the opposite direction hit him after that he really didn't remember what happened.

"Thank God. You will be yourself soon." I said and asked "What did she say finally?"

He said "it's all over I don't want to talk about this."

"Are you still in talking terms" I asked.

"No." he replied.

Karan wanted to know all about this so he convinced Ajay to share his love story with us. But Ajay was reluctant to share, but we were adamant too and finally we convinced him....

Colleges Days......!!!!!

College Days

I just completed my graduation from Pune University and was working in a small software firm as a web developer, at the same time I wanted to pursue master's degree as well, but I had noticed that attendance was compulsory in almost all the colleges, so working and studying at the same time was a bit difficult. Meanwhile, I received a call from my college and they told me to come for taking admission in masters.

I told her "Madam due to my office, I am unable to come between Monday to Friday."

"Okay, no problem come on Saturday." She replied

Saturday morning, I reached college at 10 am but found that she wasn't in her cabin so I decided to sit there and wait for her. In between I recollected old college days and never thought that once again I will be coming to the same college, but destiny has its own faith.

It was around 10.30 in the morning and madam still hasn't come to college, I decided to call her, but she didn't receive my call. So, I decided to wait for her outside since I was getting bored sitting lonely in the cabin. As soon as I came out I saw madam coming from the front.

As soon as she came, she said "sorry dear, I came a bit late because of my daughter."

"No issues. I understand." I said.

I asked her for what reason she has called me. "Come along with me to my cabin." She said.

We both went inside. "There is good news for you as our college is planning to start master's degree from this academic year. I suggest you to pursue your master's degree from our own college. There is a benefit for older students as our principal is willing to offer concession in fees for the working students. Attendance is not compulsory as they can come on every Saturday to clear their doubts." She said.

I was fascinated with this idea. It was indeed very good news.

"What will be the fee structure for this course? Do we get concession in fees? " I asked her.

"I need to check with the principal about this, after that only I will have a clear picture about this." She replied.

"If this plan rolls out well, then most of the students from our college will agree to take admission in our college for Masters. So in this way it will be a boon to our college as well. Since this is the first batch our college is willing to start, so most of the students are not aware of this." I said.

"I will check with the principal and let you know or else I will mail all of you about the fee and the course structure. I suggest you all to take admission in our college. It will be beneficial to all." She said

"I will let everyone know whoever are in touch with me." I replied

It was around 11o'clock in the morning. I left the college smiling as whatever I thought was happening and now I can work as well as pursue my masters simultaneously.

After a few days, I received a mail from the college that the admission has started, I called madam and said that it would be a bit difficult for me to come down to college on weekdays to take admission even Saturday will not be possible as work load in my office has tremendously increased.

"It's okay, I will handle this. You just send me a photograph along with fee through one of your friends, the rest I will take care of. "She said

I called one of my close friends and told him about my situation so he agreed to take admission of mine on my behalf.

Finally, my admission formalities had been completed and college was going to start from next week but due to time constraints, I was unable to attend the lectures. I was totally blank about what was going on in our college and the best part was even I didn't know how many subjects were there for this semester.

Almost after a month finally my office project was delivered. I was a bit relaxed. I decided to go to college on the coming Saturday. I was totally excited and was waiting for the Saturday for quite a long time.

Finally the day had arrived for which I was waiting for, I was really excited to go to college. It's been around 10 o'clock and lectures had already started and I was late on the very first day of my college.

I didn't know where my classroom was located. I was searching here and there for my classroom so in the mean time I wasted a few more minutes but at last I found my classroom.

"Excuse me Madam, May I come in?" I asked.

All of a sudden all these students of my class were staring at me. I was feeling a bit odd since after one month, I was attending the college that too late very first day.

"Ohhh, so finally you came to college, I thought you would be coming at the end of the semester." Sonia madam said.

All my classmates started laughing. I didn't say anything and walked inside the classroom and saw a desk empty so I sat there.

It was testing lecture going on and Sonia madam had written black box testing on the board. Before she started the lecture she asked everyone in the class "anyone of you have any idea about white and black box testing?"

There was absolute silence in the class and everyone kept mum and each one of them was staring at one another. I kept quiet and waited for some time and then took the initiative to answer Sonia's question.

As I was answering, I was not completely correct so in between Sonia Ma'am corrected me few times. All of a sudden all the students started looking at me. A few of them knew me. The rest were curious to know who this person was and since it was his first lecture how come he was able to answer the question correctly.

After some time my eyes rolled out to a girl seating in the corner silently and noting down the points. The moment I saw her I couldn't resist myself staring at her.

Her eyes were sapphire blue, skin was slightly lighter than Ivory, with a metallic rose colored tint to her cheeks. Her lips were like a frozen rose, dangerous but beautiful.

She was looking very cute and looked serious about her study. I don't know why. But looking at her I was feeling happy by heart. First time in my life I was really impressed by a girl, I don't know why but this was it.

Positive vibes were coming from inside and a couple of times I looked at her at the same time Sonia caught me. I was afraid that, madam will tell in front of the class, that stop staring at her and you do concentrate on the lecture. I was feeling ashamed but ma'am in sign language told me to concentrate on my studies so I also smiled and said "sure...!"

As soon as the lecture was over, I told Sonia madam, that I wanted to talk to her.

"Come along with me to the staff room." She said

There in the staff room, I met a lot of teachers after a very long time. I said hello to all of them. I came to know that she is our class teacher who was conducting the lecture. I wanted to discuss with her about the unit tests, after that I came out from the staff room and started looking for that girl. I didn't know her name nor anything till now. I just had a glimpse of her.

As there goes of the famous saying "Love is like Air – *Kahi bhi ho jata hai*". I think it was love at first sight and only my heart could feel it. I was going to the first floor for the next lecture and after reaching there I again started searching for her. As I was searching for her the ma'am who was supposed to conduct the lecture saw me and said "What are you doing here? You should be in the classroom."

"Yes, I was going there only" I said.

As soon as I entered the classroom, I noticed she was already seated there on the first bench. I tried to get a place around her but all the benches were occupied. So I had to move to last bench, but from there I could not see her. I was lost in my own world and found the lecture was over. I asked myself how come the lecture got over so quickly.

It was the last lecture for that day and everyone left after that. I was thinking about talking to her, but was a bit confused as what to talk to her. But I don't know whether I was right. I saw her leaving the classroom so I started following her and tried to speak to her. At the same time suddenly somebody closed my eyes from behind.

"Who was playing the prank with me?" I asked.

He asked me "Guess who's this?"

I was still lost in her thoughts and was not able to identify who the person was? He should be someone I know. He was my close friend Sumeet, who always disturbs me at the wrong time.

He was so excited after seeing me and said "At last you have come to college, I thought you would directly come to the exams."

"It's nothing like that, I just came to college only to meet you all." I said.

He said don't say anything rubbish then I asked him "So who all are the newcomers this time and from them who are the hot looking girls in our college."

"There are many this time, just tell me about whom you are talking so that I can help you with this." Sumeet said.

"There is nothing like that, in general I was asking." I said.

"By the way, who all the new guys in our class."

He gave a few names of boys and then in between I asked him who all are the new girls in our class.

He started giving few girl's names but I still didn't know the name of the girl whom I saw in my class today. I didn't bother to ask him, as he would tell everyone in our class about this and before moving ahead everything will come to a standstill.

I tried to figure out what could be her name among them. I was still searching for her, but I realized that she had left for the day.

I was still lost in her thoughts and was anxious as I will not be able to come to college the next weekday as I have my office so I can only see her next Saturday. After coming home I started searching on Facebook that Sumeet has told me, but she didn't turn up in Facebook.

I started waiting for next weekend working in office we don't realize how the weekdays came to an end. They went really fast..

Next Saturday, I went early to college around 10am. I didn't even know the lectures for that day, but sitting at home was a bit difficult for me as I was very curious to meet her. I went to the library to enquire about the lecture as well as the timetable of our class and I noticed some of our classmates have come to college. As soon as I came out of the library I saw her for whom 'my soul was searching'.

I was eager to talk to her today that in between ma'am told everyone to come inside the classroom for the lecture. As we all were moving towards the classroom then suddenly one of her friends told her to wait, but I moved forward and went into the classroom and sat on the first bench.

I saw a vacant bench beside me, I was hoping that she would sit there. She did sit on that bench.

There are some moments which you think about and suddenly they happen. After this the lecture started and everyone got involved in the lecture. I was looking at her and I noticed that again she was too involved in the lecture and noting down all the points. After the lecture was over I went near to her and said "hello" and she too said "Hello".

I asked her, "Do you have notes of all the subjects?"

"I do have a few." She replied.

"Do you have any notes currently? " I asked her again.

"I do have database." She said.

"Can you please give it to me? I will Xerox it and return it to you." I asked.

"I don't have the complete notes as soon as they are completed, I will give it to you." She said

"Okay." I said

This was the first time I was talking to her in between all this I forgot to ask her name. My friends were going to play cricket and they asked me to come along with them. But I was not in a mood to go with them. I told them that since I come only on Saturdays to college so let me attend all the lectures and then I will join you. Suddenly one of our classmates came shouting that there is no more lectures for the day as madam is on leave.

After this we all came into the corridor and again my friends started forcing me to come to play along with them since there were no more lecture for that day. She too had come in the corridor. I saw that she was talking to some of the boys of our class. I went near them to hear what they were talking about. I noticed they were talking about the boring lecture and were discussing about the drawbacks of ma'am. Which I was totally against so I interrupted and said "ma'am, might be having some personal reason she couldn't turn up today to college."

Then the same girl replied for whom I came to college "Since you don't come to college regularly, you don't know about this as this is her daily routine".

As she was saying I was just agreeing with her whatever she said as her voice was very pleasant and soothing. I asked her that we haven't introduced ourselves to each other. She said "My Name is Aastha." and she asked me "Why you don't come regularly to college."

I told her since I am working so it is not possible for me to come daily to college. She was impressed with this. My friends were continuously calling me for playing cricket, but I was not feeling to move away from her. I thought now really I need to go otherwise they are gonna kill me.

Before going I asked her "If you don't mind, can I ask you one thing?"

"Sure," She said

As I don't come to college regularly, "Can you give me your mobile number? So I can ask you about important information about the college else you can take my number and call me if anything is important for which I need to come to college."

She kept quiet for some time and was feeling shy to give her number in front of everyone but finally she gave her number.

As soon I was trying to call her to share my number, then I realize I don't have enough balance to call her.

"Ohhh, sorry yaar I do not have enough balance to call you. Do one thing you take down my number."

She was really surprised by this and said "Since you are earning and still you don't have enough balance in your mobile."

"Since morning I was quite busy so I didn't have enough time to recharge so I came to college in a hurry." I replied.

I think, it has passed two days and it was around 6.30pm, when I came back from office and messaged her "Hi"

"Hello...!!!" She replied.

"How are you?" I asked.

"I am fine, thanks..!! How about you?" She replied.

"I am good too." I replied.

I was a bit confused what to talk with her now since I didn't message her anything she also didn't reply either.

Next day, again in the evening I messaged her "Hi what are you doing?"

"Nothing great." She replied.

"What you did today?" I asked.

"As usual went to college." She replied.

"Ok, What happened today?" I said.

"Nothing great as usual lecture were conducted." She replied

I asked her "any new news for me about the college"

"No." She said

"Okay...No problem good night...talk to you later" I said. She replied me the same.

Friendship

Day Thursday,

It was around 7 o'clock in the evening, I just came from the office and saw that the current was not there. Usually this happens on Thursday. It was quite dark. I was not able to see where my things are. I was searching for my mobile since it has a torch in it. I was just moving my hands here and there in the dark in search of my mobile. Finally, I saw my mobile and soon as I was trying to turn the torch on, then I saw a notification on my mobile that a message from Aastha.

I was quite surprised and excited as well. I was totally blank as what I was up to as I read her message "Hey have you reached home?"

I was quite happy and replied her "Yes, just now." At the same time I was surprised as well how can she message me?

I texted her "How come you thought about me."

"Since from the last 2-3 days you didn't message me, I thought that if you were upset with me regarding anything." She replied.

"I was quite busy in the office so I didn't get the time to message you. By the way, for what reason I will be upset with you." I said.

"Are you coming to college coming Saturday? " She asked.

"I am not sure." I said.

"Why? " She asked.

"I have some work, so may not be able to come. " I replied.

"As you come once in a week and in that also you are avoiding to come, I suggest whatever work you have, please do it on Sunday and come on Saturday." She said.

"Okay, I will try my best. Right now going for dinner, will see you on Saturday. Good night." I replied.

I was quite excited and didn't realize when the current came back and was eagerly waiting for coming Saturday.

It was Friday night and I was eagerly waiting for Saturday morning, as I was very excited to go to college which I was never so much excited before. I was constantly looking at the watch for time to pass by. It was 5 o'clock in the morning and college was at 9 o'clock. I tried to sleep but was unable to sleep as I was very excited to meet her. I wanted to be looked more handsome of my life. It was the day of converting my dream into reality. I used the bathroom that day more than one hour. Spent half an hour in front of mirror in order to be perfect in every possible way.Icombed my hair almost 20 times and waiting for 9 o'clock. I had habit like talking with myself, reading her message again and again checking phone in every 2 minutes.

Finally, it was 9 o'clock. I was ready to leave for college. It was approximately 5km from my home so I took an auto to go to college. It took me 20 minutes to reach college and started going towards the classroom, then suddenly Aastha came towards me and said "Hi"

I suddenly turned back and replied "oh hey, I didn't see you. What a surprise?"

"So you finally came to college." She said.

"I just came to meet you." I replied.

"What?" She said.

"Nothing, I was just kidding, by the way what are the lectures for today." I asked.

"You don't have the timetable or what?" She asked.

"I haven't remembered in which book I wrote the timetable, now let it be and just tell me the lectures for today." I said and asked.

"Right now we have C++ lecture. Let's move toward the class as we are getting late." She said.

She wore an eye-catching white dress and her silky loose hair and milky shiny skin resembles like an angel.

We both started going towards the class and after reaching there we both sat together on the same bench. Every other minutes she was adjusting her silky hair, which was falling over her eyes that peaking me 'ohhhhh'. It was C++ lecture going on. I was not interested in attending the lectures rather I used to come for fun and playing pranks and most importantly for marking the attendance. The same moment she touched my hand, a swift charge run through my whole body.

I tried to play pranks and passing comments, yet was not able to do, as I saw her sitting seriously and patiently listening to the lecture. Prior to this I never went to the lecture so genuinely. Now it is diverse as I too was quietly seated and listening to the lecture. I was even unable to discover what I was up to, whatever she was doing I was willing.

After the lecture all the students went to the canteen but I used to find it very boring but as everyone says *"Everything is fair in love."* I also went along with them to the canteen.

We all sat together on the table. I was facing in front of her. They all started talking about the lecture, which I was finding really boring, but just for her I sat with them quietly and patiently listened to them. I was just looking at her the more I see her the prettier I found her every time. While she was talking, her eyes expressed her words better than her lips. She finished her words, but I understood nothing what she was trying to tell.

The worst thing among this was that these people used to go to canteen just for chatting and never order anything to eat. I was totally stuck in between as I could not leave as she would feel bad about this.

It was around 1.30 pm and time for C++ practical so everyone started going towards the practical lab. As I was quite bored, I decided to go home without informing anyone.

It was 7.30 pm when I received a message from her saying "Hi.. What are you doing?"

"I just woke up from sleep." I said.

"What? Is this the right time to sleep?" She replied.

"After coming from college, I was quite tired and feeling sleepy so I slept." I said.

"Ohhhh..Yeah, when did you leave from college, you even didn't tell me, I was searching you." She said.

"What the hell boring stuff you all were talking about in the canteen, because of which I was bored, so I left." I replied.

"Why do you find canteen as boring. We all were there and having so much fun." She said.

"As you all were talking in the local language which I am unable to understand, so I was feeling lonely. If you all can speak in English it will be much better as I too can join you and by the way I never like going to the canteen." I replied.

"Ohh sorry, from next time onwards I promise, we all will speak in English so that you will not be left out." She said.

"Okay, No problem. By the way, you must have enjoyed a lot in college today." I said

"Why?" She asked.

"Because I had come to college", I replied.

"So what's so special about this?" She said.

"As I only know how to manage time to come to college. You insist me a lot otherwise I would not have come to college." I replied.

"Ohh…that's true." She said.

"Anything else" I said.

"What?" She asked.

"Just anything what you like." I said.

"You can ask anything." She said.

What to ask as I was confused, all of a sudden I asked her which is your favorite color. She said "You guess."

"May be black and pink." I said.

"Similar type of, by the way, what's your favorite color" She asked.

"Black" I said

I think, we both were confused and unable to decide what to ask each other just pointing to each other to ask something.

She asked me "Tell me something about you."

"I think you should ask something so that I can reply." I replied.

"Tell me anything." She said.

I am a bit confused as well as clueless.

"Alright…don't say anything I am off to sleep." She said.

"Ahh are you angry with me?" I said.

"Nothing like that." She said.

"Then say something" I said.

"If you want to say something, say it fast or else it's already late in the night." She said.

"Okay, let me think" I said.

I was thinking what to say? And suddenly I said in the haste "I love you."

"??????????? What is this?" She replied

"I was just joking … !!" I said

"You really scared me from now on please don't play such pranks with me." She replied.

"I am extremely sorry if I hurt you." I said

She messaged me "Good night"

"Really my intention was not really to hurt … I am really sorry. Good night" I replied.

Next day,

I followed my daily routine i.e. Office to home, home to office. Whole day I was thinking about her that she might be really upset with me. I don't have any idea whether she will talk to me or not.

That evening I was a bit confused. Whether I should message her or not? Then I made up my mind to speak to her, in a bit of hesitation, I messaged her "Hey, what's up?" I didn't receive any reply from her so I was quite sure that she was really angry with me but after some time she replied back" Nothing as usual same routine college to home."

"What happened today in college?" I asked her.

"Nothing special as usual lectures." She said.

"Who all came to college today." I asked.

"Mostly all these students came except you." She replied.

"That's true." I replied.

"What did you do today?" She asked.

"Nothing special as I was working on a project." I replied

"By the way, what do you do?" She asked.

"I am a web developer and normally make websites." I said.

"Wow, sounds good. How much do you earn per month?" She asked.

"Not much, but sufficient enough to survive for a month." I replied.

"It's absolutely alright, if you don't want to discuss. I won't ask you about it." She said.

I was thinking that I should tell her or not, then I thought I should share with her as we both have become close friends.

"10000 per month." I replied.

"That's really great. You are stable now." She said.

"Nothing like that. Well, it's enough for pocket spending." I replied.

"Look...While studying you are earning as well... What else, do you want. This is really good. I appreciate it." She said.

This went on a daily basis, we started talking daily with each other and we were happy with it. Mostly we used to talk every night, now we became so much habitual to talk to each other daily that we can live without having food but impossible without talking to each other. Now it became such that without talking to each other, we couldn't sleep properly.

Now we both becamefamiliar with each other and started talking on a personal front.

It went for another one month and again it was Friday night and she asked me "Are you coming to college tomorrow." I replied "Don't ask me such things, I don't know whether I will be able to come or not."

"Why shouldn't I ask, you are coming tomorrow and I don't want to hear anything else." She replied.

"I am really not in a mood to come to college." I replied.

"You will have to come to college tomorrow anyhow as I have some surprise for you, so it's my order that you have to come." She said.

"What is the surprise, so that I can decide whether I should come or not." I said.

"What's the meaning of surprise then if I say everything about it right now." She replied.

"At least say something or else even a hint will do." I replied.

"I was just kidding." She said.

"Oh really." I replied.

"Yeah, I learn from you only as you alone can't play pranks even I too can" She said.

"You are too much, if we keep talking like this it will become morning." I said.

We even didn't realize and it's already 1 am. "Yes, we should sleep now. " She said.

Next day morning, I woke up hurriedly and looked at the clock and I was really shocked that it was 9 in the morning. I quickly got ready as I had to go to college. I reached college a bit late and rushed toward the classroom where I notice that lecture had already started, I tried to find a seat for myself when all of a sudden she offered me to sit beside her.

We were seated together and as usual, I was not in a mood to attend the lecture seriously. I started passing comments and make everyone laugh. Then she poked me and said "Please be quiet and be attentive in lecture."

I realized that, I have completely surrendered myself to her so whatever she says "I feel like obeying it."

Our class teacher was quietly watching this and then she asked me to stand up and explain me, what I have written on the board.

As madam told me this thing, there was pin drop silence and everyone was thinking that madam was not going to spare him this time. I started walking towards the board everyone started looking at me. I turned around and faced toward the class, made myself composed and started explaining. Everyone was shocked as how come I was able to explain and were looking at each other.

After I completed my explanation, madam was really pleased with me and said that's good but henceforth be more attentive in the class.

As soon as the lecture was over I asked her to come with me and eat something, as I was hungry. I was not quite sure whether she will come with me or not but then she agreed. It was the first time that we both were walking together and moved towards the road side stall. I was a bit hesitant to talk to her as usually we use to talk over the phone with each other. This was the first time I asked her "How did I explain in the class."

"I think, you are crazy, I was really scared that you will be punished today for sure." She said.

"How can I make this happen as I am quite well versed to explain this. It was such an easy subject, I don't find anything to learn from this." I said.

"What did you find easy in this? As I find it really difficult to grasp it." She said.

"It is useless to by heart it, always understand the concept and then answer." I said.

"What's to understand in this? As it is too difficult, you are really genius" She said.

I smiled. "Yes, I am."

At the stall, I ordered sandwiches and she initially refused to order anything but I forced her and she ordered for a glass of juice. After eating we both again went to the classroom to attend the remaining lectures.

In the evening after reaching home, I again messaged her that I want to tell her something serious.

"What? Say." She asked.

"Promise me you won't feel bad about this." I said.

"I won't, now say." She said.

I was thinking whether to say it to her or not.I was totally confused so I opened my laptop and searched on google.com *how to propose to a girl for the first time.*" I got lots of results for the same. I clicked on the first link heading as "10 Best Ways to Propose a Girl" But that makes me more confused at the end without thinking too much I said to her "I love you."

"Again, you started joking." She asked.

"This time I am really serious." I said.

"It's enough. Just stop it." She said.

"You try to understand, I am deeply in love with you." I said.

"What the hell is going on? Will you please just stop it." She said.

"I am really serious. I want to know your answer right now." I asked.

"Sorry we are just friends and nothing else." She replied.

"Are you sure? Think about it or you can take your own time." I asked.

"No, don't ask me about this again. Good night." She replied In a harsh way.

I was in a bit of tension as well as nervous at the same time. I was thinking what should I do, whether I should call her or not. The next second I realized that she stays with her family so calling her late in the night will not be appropriate.

That whole night I was in a lot of tension as what will happen now, what will she think about me. In the morning I called her, but she did not receive my call. Then I messaged her that it's absolutely okay if it's "No" from her end. "At least speak to me and don't be angry with me."

"I don't want to talk with you anymore." She replied.

"I am extremely sorry." I said.

I messed her more than 25 times after that I too became angry with her and stopped messaging her.

After two days,

"Hello" She messaged me.

I was surprised after seeing her message and was a little bit confused whether to reply her or not. After much confusion, I made up my mind to reply her. I replied "Hey".

"What are you doing?" She said.

"Nothing." I said.

"Since you didn't message from the last two days and not even called me. I was missing you. After thinking a lot about this I came to the conclusion that I am in love with you too." She said

Even I was quite amused after reading this, but equally happy at the same time after reading this and felt like I am on cloud nine.

"Oh really or are you kidding. I don't believe this." I replied.

"What should I do in order to prove my love for you. Order me something and I will do it for you." She replied.

"That's enough in order to prove your unconditional love for me. I am really speechless at this moment." I said.

I was really happy and quite excited to meet her as she was my first love. I was quite eager to meet her from within but since it was too late in the night so I couldn't go to her home to meet her.

I messaged her that we will meet tomorrow. She replied to me "How can we meet since you will have office tomorrow." I replied "leave it to me, I will manage."

Date

Next day early morning, I messaged my boss since I am having some personal work today. I will not be able to come to the office. His reply came, "Okay, no problem."

I messaged her "I have taken leave from office so that we can meet and spend some quality time with each other. Can you meet me outside today? "

"Can you come to college so that we both can meet?" She replied.

"As you know I don't like coming to college." I replied.

"Since we have one or two important lectures, which I don't want to miss.That's why I am asking you to come college" She said.

"Oh come on, come out of this boredom college and let's meet somewhere else or maybe we can have lunch together today and please I request you to come in salwaar kameez as you look pretty cute in this" I replied.

After insisting her a lot, She finally agreed to meet outside and replied "Where do we have to meet and on what time?"

I replied "Give me some time I will think about it and let you know." After thinking for some time, I came to know that there is a good restaurant in way of her home and mine. It will be nice to meet there.

I messaged her name of the restaurant where we both can meet. She was reluctant to meet there and she said "everyone knows me in that area so I will be little bit uncomfortable to meet you there, I suggest that we meet somewhere else."

"Okay, fine then you suggests me the place." I replied.

"Will meet at Signature restaurant that is near your home. Is it fine with you?" She asked.

"Yes sure, no problem." I said.

I searched for the contact number for the restaurant on the internet and after searching it immediately I called the restaurant and told them to reserve one table for us.

As soon as I reached there she too had come at the same time and is parking her vehicle. She was wearing pink color salwaar blue kameez. She was looking hot in that dress.

"Didn't you bring your sunglasses with you?" She asked.

"Oh, I really forgot to carry them with me." I replied.

We went inside the restaurant, there a doorman was standing, who opened the door for us and we both went inside. There I saw a waiter and asked him about the reserved table which I had booked over the phone to which he said, "Sir, Could you please tell me your table number so that I can assist you."

"Table number 21." I replied.

"Okay, come along with me." He said.

We both followed him and he took us to table no 21. It was in the corner. We sat on the table and the waiter brought the menu card for us. I forwarded the menu card to her and said, " look at it and say what you want to order."

"No. You order it." She said.

"Okay. What will you have in the starter as I can see from the menu that they serve a lot of starters like Pannir tikka, masala papad, soup etc." I said.

"Whatever you like from this, you please order it. I will share it with you." She said.

I called the waiter and told him to bring the tomato soup for both of us. Then the waiter asked us "What will you like to have for the main course".

"As of now, please bring tomato soup and let me think about what to order." I said.

"Sure, sir." Waiter said and went back.

I asked her what she would like to have for the main course.

"You order anything." Again she said.

"Since I ordered the starter now it's your turn to order the main course. Don't feel shy and order anything whatever you like." I said.

She decided and said "She would like to have Punjabi food."

I called the waiter and said "How much more time it will take for the starter to come."

"They are almost done and I am just bringing it." Waiter said.

"Okay, by the time please take down the main course." I said

In the meantime, I told her that since we both have come so close to each other that too through message only. And we both had very less conversation face to face with each other.

I asked her "Say something", but she was feeling very shy to talk.

"This is my first time that I have come out to have lunch with a guy so I am a bit nervous" She said. "Don't be, same here." I replied.

"Where did you complete graduation from?" I asked her.

"Brighton college Pune" She replied.

"Okay. How was that college?" I asked.

"Overall, it was good, but somewhat it was strict." She replied.

"Alright. Tell me something about yourself or about your family." I asked.

"Well, we are three sisters. The elder sister is happily married and the middle one is already engaged. My father is working in a bank, Mother is a lecturer." She replied.

"That's great." I said.

As we were talking, the waiter came and said "Your starter has come should I serve you in two different plates or should I make it in one."

"Do one thing, put it in a single plate." She replied.

As we were eating, she asked me "Now you tell me about your family."

"I have four members in my family, my father is a government employee, mother is a homemaker and younger brother in 10th class." I said.

"Wow. Small family, happy family." She said.

"How did you like the starter?" I asked.

"It is really very tasty and tempting." She replied.

Waiter came and said, "Your main course is ready, should I bring it? "

"Yes." She replied.

The waiter was finding little bit difficult to serve us. He told us to move aside. We both were thinking about each other so didn't realize what the waiter was telling.

After some time, Aastha asked me, "Where do you work? And in which company."

"It's a small scale firm located near NIBM (National institute of bank management.)" I replied.

We both were eating as well as talking. She asked me "From how long are you working."

"Since the past one year. "I replied.

"Do you want to order something else." I asked.

"It's enough for me. If you want to order something for you, you please go ahead" She said.

"I am ordering Fruit salad. Will you share along with me?" I asked.

"No." She said.

"Can I ask you something?" She said.

I eagerly said, "Yes, please."

"Do you smoke?" She asked.

"No. Why did you ask?" I replied and asked.

"I really hate smokers." She said.

We were done with our lunch. When the waiter came and asked, "Sir, would you like to have something else or should I bring the bill?"

"Bring the bill." I said.

The waiter came with the bill. "Do you accept cards" I asked.

"Yes sir. We do." Waiter said.

I gave him my card to swipe, after some time he came along with my card. Also I gave him some tip. We both came out of the hotel. Aastha told me "It's 3 pm where we have to go."

"Let us do one thing. Come with me to my home." I replied.

"What will we do there?" She asked.

"It's very hot outside. Will take rest for some time, either we will watch the movie or will chat with each other." I said.

"Okay." She said.

My home was nearby the hotel and this was the first time she was coming to my home. As we entered into my society premises she really liked it and said "Wow, your society is very clean and beautiful. Since how long do you live here?"

"From the time I came to Pune. I am staying here. I think from around the past 5 years." I said.

After this we both reached at my doorstep and then I suddenly realized that I haven't cleaned my home in the morning today. It was all messed up. I told her to stay outside for some time in between I quickly clean the home.

"Okay." She said.

I quickly went inside and cleaned the home and then told her to come inside.

I asked her for water and after that I switched on the tv, on which an interesting film was going on so we both started to watch it. Once the movie ended, it was quite late in the evening and then Aastha told me "I am getting late and have to leave now."

"Okay." I replied.

She went down, started her vehicle and waved to me. I was standing in my balcony looking at her and I too waved her.

She messaged me after sometime "I have reached home safely."

"Alright. We will talk later, Bye for now." I replied.

"Bye" She replied.

Kiss

March 10,

I was going back home from office in a bus, and I received call from Aastha saying "Hi Jaan, have you reached home?"

"No, I haven't reached home as of now. There is lots of traffic on the road so I am stuck in it. It will take some more time to reach home." I said.

"Alright." she said.

"What happened?" I asked.

"Nothing special, just casually called you. " She said.

"Are you missing me?" I asked.

"Yes Jaan, I am really missing you so much." She replied.

"How come you are calling me at this time, are your parent's not at your home?" I asked.

"They have gone out to watch a movie." She replied.

"You too should have gone with them." I said.

"You just keep quiet, you never have time for me. Have you asked me ever for a movie? You are always busy with your office work." She said.

I didn't have any answer to her question. She angrily cut the call. I tried calling her but she was not receiving my call.

I messaged her "Jaan please receive my call." After trying to call her for 2-3 times, finally she received my call.

I said, "Jaan, why are you angry with me so much, you know very well that I have lots of work in office and that too which is in very critical condition, also you can't come out from your home on Sunday. Please try to understand my situation. We will definitely go out this coming Saturday, I promise."

"Do whatever you want to do, I don't care. It's better not to talk to you." She said.

"Why? What happened?" I asked.

Again the phone was hanged up by her, but this time I didn't call back. I guess, she was testing me whether I remember her birthday or not, if yes then what is the plan for tomorrow.

I understood what she was trying to tell me so I didn't call her back.

After reaching home, I was still thinking how to make her birthday more special. I was thinking about a lot of ideas but was unable to find anyone as every idea, which I thought seems old.

I was thinking about this from quite a long time, but not yet finalized anything. Finally, I got one idea, but it took me a lot of time to think about this. It was 10.30 at night.

As usual, till now I didn't receive any message from her, I knew that she was very angry with me, that's why she didn't message me.

I was very tired and was feeling sleepy, but I have to be awake till 12am as it was her birthday. I was thinking to set alarm and sleep for some time but then thought it would be risky as if I don't get up on time and wish her. She will kill me tomorrow. So I decided to watch movie till then.

Two minutes were remaining for 12 in the night. My heart was beating very fast. I called her; the phone's bell was tickling in ears. I was in a bit of confusion as how to wish her. At last it's was midnight and she received my call.

"Hello" She said.

"Hey Jaan, were you sleeping?" I asked.

"No" She said.

I wished her "Happy Birthday Jaan." She replied "Thank you so much."

"I am disconnecting your call as everybody is at home. We will chat through message." She said.

I then messaged her "Once again, wish you very happy birthday and love you a lot."

"Thank you very much my Jaan. Love you too my cute little rat." She replied.

Sometimes she used to call me rat affectionately. There was too much restriction at her home, but just for the sake of me she received my call.

She replied, "I knew you would be the first person to wish me on my birthday."

"Even I knew that you will be waiting for me." I replied.

"How come?" She asked.

"Might be just for the sake of love", I replied.

"Alright try to come to my home early tomorrow.", I said.

"Why so?" She asked.

"There is one surprise for you?" I said.

"Are you on leave tomorrow?" She asked.

"What did you think?" I said.

"I thought that you love your office only. How can you miss your office?" She said.

"Alright, please don't come tomorrow. I will go to my office." I replied.

"What happened, my sweet rat? Are you angry with me?" She asked.

I didn't reply for some time, she was continuously messaging me saying "She was just kidding with me. I messaged her "Alright try to come early tomorrow."

"I am not feeling like sleeping tonight." She said.

"I can understand." I replied.

"I am feeling like meeting you right now." She said.

"Wow, that sounds good, if you say then I can come right now." I asked.

"Please come." She replied

"I will come for sure right now, but do not tell me anything afterwards. You need to come down in your society once I reach there." I replied.

"What should I tell you my dear, you know everything, I too am feeling like meeting you now as I am missing you very much, really love you a lot, but due to some restriction I will not able to come down." She said.

"Love you too. Anyways we are going to meet tomorrow. It's a matter of just another 5-6 hours. Now we should sleep and will try to come in each other's dream." I replied.

"No, I want to meet you right now." She said.

"Try to understand Jaan. It's very late in the night so please try to sleep as of now, also try to come early tomorrow. I will be eagerly waiting for you from early morning."

"Okay, good night. " She said.

"Good night." I replied.

Birthday (11 March),

Finally, that day has come true for which I was waiting. I had a lot of preparation for the birthday. I woke up early. I went to gift item shop and purchased some heart shaped balloons as well as some decorating stuff.

I came back home and started decorating the inside room with the decorating stuff which I brought and with the balloons, also I wrote love quote on each balloon.

As we know if we are enjoying to the fullest and involved in. Work that you like so much, you never realize how time passes by.

It was 10.30 am. She could be coming at any time. I was not yet ready and if she comes now then everything will go waste. But I knew that she has a habit of coming little bit late, that's why I was relaxed little bit. After getting ready quickly, I was trying to call her that suddenly someone rang the doorbell.

I was quite confident that she came. When I opened the door, she was there.

She was wearing a top and jeans. She was undoubtedly looking the most beautiful, fair skin, hazel eyes, beautifully drafted nose, sweet voice… In short she was a blend of everything. A perfect Girl. She was just standing at the door and I was simply staring at her

"Won't you stop staring at me? Will you not ask me to come inside." She said

"Oh!, I am extremely sorry. Please come inside. Should I tell you one thing. You are looking very hot and I am feeling like keep looking at you". I said.

"Okay, now stop flirting with me." She said

"Leave this and look. What time you were supposed to come and what time you came?" I said.

She sat on the sofa and I was standing beside her, I held her hand and told her "Come along with me."

"Why?" She asked.

Now look here, whatever I say to you now, just comply with it. I told her to close her eyes but she was not trying to listen. I asked her to promise me to listen me so she had no other option but to follow my instruction. I was trying to cover her eyes with a small band.

"What are you doing Ajay?" She asked.

"Please hold for a while" I said.

Now she was not able to see anything. I took her along with me to another room where I have decorated. She too was quite excited and continuously telling me "Should I remove my band now?"

It was completely dark in the room, I started lighting the candles after that I told her to remove her band from her eyes. After removing the band, for a moment she just simply stared all around the room and became very emotional and speechless. I can read from her eyes. What she was trying to say, I too had become very emotional as I could understand her feelings. She was about to cry that suddenly she hugged me tightly.

It was such a moment that we both were understanding each other without saying anything. Finally, I said to her, "Let's cut the cake my dear."

I was trying to capture her photo while cutting the cake. She said that we both will cut the cake together. I told her "It's your birthday, you should cut the cake."

She said "No just keep the camera away and come near to me. There is some moment which needs to be captured in the heart rather than camera."

I sat beside her and we both cut the cake together, after that I gave her a bite to eat and she did the same.

Suddenly we came very close to each other and I stared into her eyes and my hands caressed her cheeks. My right thumb moved around her soft lips as her eyes were glued to mine.She didn't say anything, and for me it was a good sign. So I leaned down forward and paused just before I could touch her lips. I saw, she had closed her eyes and that was all the permission I needed.

Our lips meet. At first I could feel the tenderness, then she grabbed me by my hair pulling me towards her in a sudden move of passion. She opened her mouth, just enough for our tongues to interlock and do the dance.

I guess this was the first time for both of us. As we touch each other lips there was some different feeling coming within, but whatever was happening, we both were liking very much.

I felt like, "If this is what is known as heaven, then indeed it is."

Lavasa trip

We were planning to go for an outing from quite a long time so we can spend some quality time with each other. Due to some other reason we were not able to go out together.

This was mostly because of me as my project was in very critical condition, due to that I had to go to the office even on weekends.

I was fed up of going to the office every Saturday because even we use to not get any comp off for coming on weekends and only lunched served free for that day that too of our boring canteen, which I use to not like.

If you use to ask for a comp off, then every time we use to get the same reply "Cost of the project is very low, we can't afford it."

I was helpless as if I didn't go on Saturday the project will be escalated.

Everyone was fed up with that project as when it's SIT (System integration testing) and UAT (User acceptance testing) will end up.

Mostly during weekends, nobody was in the mood to work compared to weekdays, but due to the strict guideline from our manager we have to come, just for the sake of attendance.

As everyone says, if you dislike a particular work there is better not to do that, but here the situation was reversed as we were forced to come on Saturday to work.

From the past 2 months we were continuously coming to work on Saturdays, which means meeting my love was a bit difficult task for me.

On Sundays she couldn't come out to meet me and for me this was the only day when I use to be free.

She use to angry with me because of my office schedule. I was helpless as I could do nothing, sometimes handling the situation was a little bit tough for me.

I tried to talk my manager regarding giving us off on Saturdays, but he was not willing to listen and at the same time Aastha did not want to hear anything related to my office.

It was high time and everyone decided that from coming Saturday, no one will go to the office, if everyone is united and firm on their decision even management has to budge down.

As soon as I received a message that from this coming Saturday we will be getting weekly off. I was very happy. The first thing which I did after this was to call Aastha and tell her that I have a holiday from next Saturday, we can plan to go on coming Saturday.

She said angrily "I don't want to go anywhere, if you want to go, you go or else do one thing go to office."

"I have a holiday this Saturday didn't you listen properly." I replied.

"Then also you go to the office." She said.

I tried my best to make her understand. She was not willing to hear me. She was still very angry with me. I continuously messaged her, but neither she was replying to my message nor she was receiving my calls.

At some point I think, she was right. I was in such a situation in which I was helpless. I was not able to do anything, neither she was willing to understand.

It was Saturday morning, I was still unable to understand what to do and then all of a sudden one idea clicked me that I should go to her home but at the same time, I was feeling scared that if her parents are at home, "What they will think about it." What will I say to them as to which purpose I have come? As I heard from her that her parents is too strict. They don't like if she talks or spend time with any unknown boy. Of course Aastha hasn't introduced me to his parents soAfter all if they will ask me who are you? What will I answer them?

After much hesitation, I finally decided to go. I was little bit assured that her parents might have gone to office so probably she will be alone at home. Her parents usually used to go to the office on around 10.30 am.

I reached near to her home, my heart was beating fast, as who will be at her home at this time. I was trying to ring her doorbell, was unable to do because of nervousness, at last finally I did ring the bell.

When the door opened, she was standing in front of me and finally I could get hold of myself.

She went inside without saying anything. I realized that nobody is there at her home and felt relaxed. Thinking for a while followed her inside by locking the door.

She was in the kitchen doing some work, looking at her I felt that she was still angry. I went close to her and said "Hello"

She didn't reply. I hold her from back and said, "Jaan why are you angry with me, say something."

She was not willing to say anything.

"Please try to understand and say something, I purposefully didn't do it. I am extremely sorry if I hurt you in any way." I said.

She was refusing to listen me even after explaining my situation. I hold my ears with my hand and started doing squats and told her that till the time she doesn't forgive me, I will continue to do this.

I started doing this and after doing around 35 - 40 times. I was feeling pain and discomfort, but I stood by my decision and continue doing this even with pain and discomfort.

She could easily see this from my face. Finally she holds and told me to stop. As soon as she said this I was happy that finally she said something.

As I stood up from squats, she hugged me tightly and said "How much do you trouble me, you know, how much I missed you."

"I agree with you. The fact is that you too trouble me a lot." I said.

She smiled and asked me, "Have you eaten something?"

"No, after waking up directly came here." I said

"What will you have?" She asked.

"Usually in the office, I have porridge every day for breakfast so I am used to it. Do one thing you make porridge." I said.

I knew, you will say this. She started making porridge. I was helping her. She had calmed down. I said to myself "Thank god. Finally, she agreed."

I was thinking how to tell her that I am thinking to take her out somewhere, but was scared at the same time that the same topic will start and she will get angry with me again. I decided to keep quiet and not to say anything.

We both had porridge together. It was around 12 o'clock in the afternoon.

I asked her," Will you come along with me outside for lunch?"

"No. My mom is supposed to come in another hour I suggest it will be waste going outside rather we can spend time together at my home only." She replied.

"Okay, at the same time I told her that we will be going out on Monday together." I said.

"Monday???????? What about your office?" She replied.

"I know, but I have taken leave on Monday." I said.

"Oh really you have taken leave on Monday. I can't believe it." She said.

She was really very excited. I was in confusion as where to take her as I was unable to decide. After much discussion, we finally decided that we will go to Lavasa.

Lavasa is around 30km from Pune city in Maharashtra state, situated on hill top having pleasant climate and picturesque location. I never went there neither did she before, so we decided to go there.

It was Monday morning. I was quite excited to go to Lavasa and on top of that going with her made me very happy. I woke up at 8.30am and our plan was to leave by 9.30am for Lavasa. I got ready very quickly and started waiting for her. The climate was also very pleasant and it was looking like that it was going to rain.

I had been waiting since thirty minutes and it looked like I was waiting there since forever. I started to hear my heart beating.

As usual, she came very late around 10am, at that time it started raining. She was little bit wet by the time she reached my home. She turned around and closed her eyes, letting her head be drenched from the falling water, flattening her hair to her skin.As she ran her hands through her hair, listening to the water hit the cold stone, soft skin was pressed against her lips allowing the water to trickle around them.It was quite romantic also the rain was increasing slowly into high showers

We started moving towards Lavasa from my home, by that time it was raining heavily. We were almost wet, as this was the first time I had come with her for fun and that too during rainy season but to enjoy and get wet in rainfall with someone special is a different feeling altogether.

The road was peopled with giant trees.I could feel the puff of rain blowing over my cheeks. I realized not that it was a roundabout ahead and that I was supposed to take a turn. I narrowly escaped an accident.

At the same time we were scared as both of us have not said anything in our family. She was continuously telling me to drive slowly as we were moving ahead the rain was increasing and it had become very cloudy, because of that I was not able to see properly too.

A few days before landslide incident has occurred in Uttrakhand and somewhat like that situation, it seems would happen here. The road leading to Lavasa was quite narrow and lonely with many potholes. It was cloudy weather because of which it had become very dark.

I was feeling like that we two only are there in this world because of the situation we were in, at the same time it made us excited as well.

It was around another one km. left to reach Lavasa. We felt that there will surely be a cloud burst so we were really scared to move ahead.

We decided to park our bikes there itself and finally we were feeling "We are at the top of the world. Where apart from us nobody is there."

I said to her, "Close your eyes."

"Why?" She asked.

"Please do it." I said.

I saw a bunch of flowers around. I plucked one flower and went on my knees in front of her and in a polite voice told her "Jaan, open your eyes."

As soon as she opened her eyes. She was shocked and surprised to see me in such a position. I proposed her and said "Will you marry me?" In no time she said "Yes."

As soon as I heard "I couldn't control myself I just kissed her on forehead and hold her hand and said "*I Promise you we will walk together till the life ended.*"

She was speechless and unable to say anything but I could understand from her body language. How much happier she was.

As everyone says that "*Only heart can read another heart.*"

She grasped me, by the time the rain had slowed down. We could hear the chirping of the bird. It was a hush around us. The earth was very serene and wonderful. I think it was the most beautiful moment of my life.

It was around 2pm. I asked her, "Should we go ahead?"

"Actually I think, I am getting late to reach home. We have to leave. Frankly speaking, I am in no mood to go home. I am thinking of staying back with you and start our household here. There is no one here only you and me and this beautiful moment with us. But what to do I am helpless. "She replied.

I said to her, "Wait for some time we will definitely make our home at such place."

We started heading back home.

One night with her

There is trend in IT industry as every employee waits anxiously for Friday as there is weekend after it, so everyone has a plan in place to enjoy it. Like others I too used to wait for Friday on my calendar, but I would say I was a bit more curious as only on Saturdays I could meet my sweetheart.

It was Friday afternoon, I went to the office canteen to have lunch. I saw my friends already waiting there for me with my seat reserved as during lunch time the office canteen gets crowded and whoever comes first would reserve the seats for their friends.

I took my plate and sat along with my friends. We use to have a gala time during lunch hours as this was the time when we used to sit together and enjoy each other's company.

Mostly everyone was fed up with the food served in the canteen as we use to think, there is no difference between the food which is served in the canteen and hospital. There were two or three folks who used to bring home made food and would share with us.

Mostly it would happen that we only would eat up all homemade food and they would get nothing except the same canteen boring food.

As we were eating, my mobile started to vibrate but I could not realize it, as I was busy in eating. My friend who was sitting beside me told everyone that someone's mobile is vibrating.

I told him that I too felt so. And then my friend came to know that it was none other than my mobile which was vibrating. I too realized that it was indeed my phone. This used to happen mostly because of loud noise in the canteen during lunch hours.

I took out my mobile from my pocket and saw that it was my love's call, in between one of my friends told that receive "Babhiji's call."

I was a bit shocked as why she is calling me at this time. I received her call but couldn't hear properly what she was trying to say as there was a lot of disturbance there.

I told her that I will call you back after my lunch.

"It's okay, but do call me back without fail." She said.

I got worried as why she told me to call her back without fail. Also she does call me at this time around. I quickly gobbled my food and then called her.

"Hi Jaan, say what happened?" I asked.

"Till what time will you come back from office?" She asked.

"Why? You know at what time I come back, then why are you asking me again." I said.

"Yes, I know it. Still what time will you come back today" She asked.

I was getting a little bit irritated because of her constantly asking the same question again and again.

I told her that I would be getting late tonight as I will be leaving around 9pm from office. It will take me an hour to reach home.

"Why, so late. Do you have lot of work in office? Can't you try to come a little bit early today?" She asked.

"Why? What happened?" I asked.

"You have to come early tonight. It's my order, I have got some surprise for you, call me once you reach home." She said.

"Oh! gosh, how much do you play with me, at least sometimes say something instead of giving me clues." I said.

"If I tell you right now then it won't be a surprise anymore." She replied.

"Alright, I will try and will confirm you about the timing." I said and disconnected the phone.

I was thinking about her surprise as what could be in store for me. Till now she never called me so late in the night, now all of a sudden she is calling me. I was totally blank as what surprise she is going to give me.

I was having a lot of work in the office. Usually it happens that whenever I wanted to leave early that day only work load would increase. I was planning to leave by 6.15pm office bus so decided to wrap up all my work by 5.30pm so that I could report to my manager till 5.40pm.

After planning, I started my work, everything was going according to plan, I wrapped up my work and came down to catch my bus. I searched for my route bus and then sat inside. It takes me around 1 hour 20 minutes to reach home.

Usually I use to get inside the bus 2 minutes before the departure time as everyone used to gather around the bus and discuss with each other about their project work and latest news in their cluster. Among this some peoplecome early just to stare at hot and beautiful girls and try to flirt with them.

In Pune Hinjewadi area is a prime location, mostly known as IT hub, most famous for its heavy traffic. Crossing the heavy traffic of Hinjewadi was like walking at a snail's pace. We used to get very bored sitting in the bus for long hours.

Some people used to listen local FM, but now days it was also very boring because of repeating songs and advertisements.

I guess that they were not so bad days as there was some excitement involved in it. I used to sleep late at night so getting up early in the morning was quite difficult for me, so mostly I used to go running to the pickup location or sometimes used to call my office colleague in the bus and tell him to wait for some time.

Sometimes it could happen that I did not get time to pin up my shirt buttons also sometimes I used to tie my shoe lace in the bus due to hurry.

It was 7pm. I was still in the bus waiting to reach home, at the same time Aastha was messaging me continuously as where the bus was and what time it will reach.

"Still, I am in the bus, will reach home in some time and will get fresh." I replied.

"Where do we have to meet?" I asked.

There was a burger outlet near her home. Where we used to meet quite often. She told me to meet at the burger outlet.

"Alright. I will be there in 20 min." I said.

As promised, I reached at the venue at the said time and messaged her "Where are you? I have reached."

I didn't receive any reply from her. I thought probably she might be driving. Her home was about 5-8 minutes drive from here. I expected her to reach here by this time.

Around 7.40pm she finally reached. As soon as she reached I was looking at my watch, she thought that she was too late and then said sorry to me.

No matter, how angry I get with her sometimes, but looking at her innocent face my anger gets vanished.

"You look very tired today, did you have more work load today?" She asked.

"Yeah, a little bit tired, what is the surprise and where we have to go." I asked

"You have to come along with me to my home. My parents are waiting to meet you." She said.

"What?????? Why are they waiting to meet me? If you would have said this to me before I would have come smartly dressed, just look at me how shabby I am looking. This is too much, you are just going to kill me tonight" I said.

"You have to deal with the situation. I have already told you before that I am going to give you a surprise, you should have prepared for it." She said.

"Are you supporting me or pulling my leg? Just tell me frankly, how I am looking or else I will do one thing. I will quickly go home get ready and come back." I said.

"Leave it. Just come with me now quickly as I told them that I will bring you along with me." She said.

"Okay, what should I say to them? Why they want to meet me."

"I am worried and you are not telling me anything. By the way tell me one thing after meeting them what should I do. Should I say them "Namaste" or Should I touch their feet and take their blessing" I asked.

"Do what you wish." She said.

This reminded me of a film sequence and I went to a flashback "How should I greet them, should I say hello or Namaste. Should I touch their feet or just a formal handshake?" I was totally confused.

I was very much tense as why they wanted to meet me, as this was the first time I was going to meet them. I felt that I was not properly dressed; my hair was quite long and was looking quite dull from my face because of tiredness.

I never expected that in such a situation, I would be meeting her parents. I was also quite angry with Aastha. We reached her parking place. She used to stay at 3rd floor. We started heading towards her home.

I again asked her "Jaan, Please tell me. Why they want to meet me also what should I say to them".

"Be calm and confident and just reply to what they ask." She said.

Alright, I started walking with her. I was standing in front of the door and I was feeling like I was in the KBC game show sitting on the hot seat with Mr. Amitabh Bachchan standing in front of me. As she was removing the door keys I asked her "Is the current not there? Why are you not ringing the doorbell?"

"Why to disturb them? I will open the door." She said.

She removed the door key from her purse and then opened the door. It was completely dark in her home with only a candle burning. I started thinking quickly. What could be the reason behind this, as also it was not my birthday. I was totally blank as what was happening. I also could not see her parents anywhere around.

I asked her, "Where are your parents? She pointed her fingers and said they might be in the other room." I sat on the sofa prepared to impress them and told her to call her parents. She was smiling.

I felt something fishy and realized that there was nobody in the house except us, still was not clear about it. She went inside the other room started laughing at that time I realized that she was playing prank on me. I followed her in the other room and after seeing me she started laughing even louder that time I realized there was really nobody in the room.

I again asked her "Where are your parents, please tell me and stop laughing." She smiled and said "They might have gone downstairs and will come back shortly." Alright, let them come till that time I will wait for them.

As I was coming out of the room, she held my hand and said, "My dear Jaan. How innocent are you."

"Yeah, I too know that your parents are not here and they are not going to come back." I replied.

"Well then you are smart" She said.

"Yes, I am. Where have they gone?" I asked

"My mother was having some college work in Kolhapur (District near Pune). She went there along with my dad and they will be coming tomorrow." She said.

"Okay, will you be staying alone tonight, don't you feel scared." I asked.

"Where are you going? You are going to stay here till the time they come." She said.

"You are totally crazy." I said.

"Why?" she asked.

"As you knew everything, why didn't you say directly to me all this instead of fooling me." I said.

"I like to play pranks with you." She said.

"Yeah, I know. You are going to really kill me one day. Now what should I wear." I asked.

"You can try my T-shirt." She said.

"What??? You are so fat how can I adjust in your T-shirt." I said.

"Then stay as you are. I don't know. Now I won't give you anything." She said angrily.

"I was just kidding Jaan." I said.

"Well, I was doing the same." She said.

"Jokes apart. Please give me your T-shirt. I really need it." I said.

She was not willing to give me, but after persuading her a lot, she finally agreed. I finally put on the T-shirt given by her.

"You can rest for a while or watch TV, meanwhile I will just wrap up some work from downstairs and come." She said.

"Can I come with you?" I asked

"No, you look tired, please take rest. I will quickly go down and come back." She said.

"Okay." I said.

As soon as I laid down on the bed, I didn't realize when I went off to sleep. I was in sleep when Aastha came hurriedly and tried to wake me up. I was still in sleep when I told her to just let me sleep for some more time. I guess it was early morning and she came to me and said, "How much will you sleep. Please get up fast. I am getting worried, my maid is standing at the door and ringing the doorbell.

I hurriedly woke up and asked, "What should I do now?"

"You hide in the washroom and let me handle the maid." She said.

"Didn't you inform her not to come today?" I asked.

"I did, but I don't know why she came. Please go fast, don't waste time. Let me ask her why she came in spite of telling her not to come." She said.

"What? In the washroom, I have to hide? Didn't you find any other place except this." I said.

"Don't think so much. Do what I say, there is not much time. " She said.

"Okay." I said.

Aastha went and opened the door and asked the maid " What happened? I told you not to come today as nobody will be home. I was just leaving outside."

"I was just passing by from here. I remembered that I forgot my umbrella at your home." Maid said.

"Where have you kept your umbrella?" Aastha asked.

"I don't really remember where I kept. Let me check in the balcony." Maid said.

"Okay... hurry up." Aastha said.

She quickly went into the balcony to find her umbrella. It was not there. "I don't find my umbrella here. It might be in the kitchen and washroom." Maid said.

Aastha in a fumbled voice said, "Washroom? I don't think it is there, I just came from there."

"Just let me check once." Maid said.

Aastha was pretty confused what she should do now as if she would continuously refrain the maid from going inside the washroom. She will find something fishy in this. As the maid was going towards the washroom both of our heartbeats were racing.

As soon as Aastha opened the door, I woke up from my sleep. I saw that Aastha has closed the door and locking it from inside. Then I realized that it was a very bad dream. Aastha looked at me and asked, "Why are you looking so frightened?"

"Nothing." I said.

She went in the kitchen and started cooking for both of us. It was around 10pm. When we both had our dinner together and started watching her favorite TV serial "Diya aur baati hum". I finished my food and asked her

"I am feeling sleepy? Where should I sleep?"

"You go inside and sleep. I will join you after watching this serial." She replied.

After watching the serial she came inside the bedroom. I gave her a pillow to sleep beside me. She refused to take it. Actually, she wanted to sleep on my arms.

"I am feeling very good sleeping along with you." She said.

It was my first night with her. She asked, "How are you feeling. Aren't you finding it something new? "

"Spending time with you makes me feel quite happy. I don't expect anything more than this. I wish you sleep along with me on my arms like this forever." I said.

"Me too" She said.

"I want to ask you one thing. Why were you scared when I came back." I shared with her what I was dreaming.

She laughed and said, "Don't worry, nothing sort of this will happen, in the worst case if it does happen I will handle it easily. By the way I have informed her not to come."

"Now you relax and sleep peacefully. So that we can cherish this moment for the life time."

Diwali

Pune, Maharashtra. In Pune Diwali is celebrated on a very large scale with great dignity and pride. In Maharashtra mainly two festivals celebrated widely, they are "Ganesh Puja and Diwali." Here for Diwali mostly there are holidays for about 10 days.

This Diwali was special for me as Aastha had invited me to her house to meet her parents and celebrate Diwali together.

As we all know that Diwali is celebrated all over India widely, but in Maharashtra people are really more enthusiastic and they start celebrating the festival prior to the actual day by bursting crackers. Especially kids over here are very naughty and mischievous. They are quite involved in bursting crackers the whole day.

This time I too got involved with the kids over here and bursted crackers with them, but at the same time I was concerned for the mother earth as bursting crackers causes a lot of air pollution, but Diwali festival creates such an environment that one is unable to resist himself.

Since this was Diwali eve and also people were bursting crackers all around. I thought for a while as people had got involved so much prior to the Diwali so what will happen on the Diwali day.

At the same time I received a message from Aastha "Be cautious and careful while bursting crackers."

"I will definitely follow your orders, will text you after some time." I replied

I got involved in bursting crackers with the kids from my society. It was around 10.30 at night and tomorrow was the Diwali. I was quite excited about this, but beyond that I was excited to go to Aastha's home. That whole night I was thinking about what to wear tomorrow, how to talk to her parents and all such stuff.

The next morning, when I woke up, I heard that people were performing Puja in the temple and ringing the bell, a pleasant smell of incense sticks was coming. When I saw wall clock, it was 8 o'clock in the morning. I thought how lazy I was, as this is Diwali and also I am getting up so late.

I quickly got ready and went to the temple, performed Puja and met all the people of the society, who were equally excited to celebrate it.

It was 6 o'clock in the evening, all the people were lighting Diya's in front of their houses. I too did it and after that everyone assembled on the terrace. On reaching porch I felt like Diwali without a doubt by watching nearby view. Wherever I could see there were vivid lights and Diya's lit all around.

Looking at the sky, it had become colorful by bursting of crackers and I was quite happy after seeing this.

It was around 8pm. I received a message from Aastha "You please come down to my house."

"I will be reaching in a while, what should I wear? What would you like me to wear?" I replied and asked.

"Whatever you like, you wear and be at your best." She replied.

I was quite nervous at the same time was confident as well. When I reached her home, I called her and said "I am in your parking place. Should I come there?"

"Yes, come fast." She replied.

Her flat was on the 3rd floor. When I reached she was already standing at her door, probably waiting for me.

As we were staring each other in between she smiled and said "Wow you are looking handsome."

Once I entered her house her parents were seating on the couch. I went near them touch their feet and took their blessing, her parents told me to sit.

I was feeling like that I had come for an interview and Aastha's parent are going to conduct my interview.

Her father asked me "How are you? How is everything going? In which company are you currently working?"

"I am fine. Thank you. How is everything with you? Previously I was working with Ainsworths Pvt. Ltd. but few days back I started working with Capgemini." I said.

He smiled and said "Wow, that's great." I smiled too.

"What is your current CTC?" He asked.

"Now, its 8 lacks. Pa." I said

Her father asked me about my family as how is everything there, what does my father do and how many siblings I have.

"I have 4 members in my house, my mom, dad and my younger brother. Dad is a government employee, mom is house wife and younger brother is in 10th class." I said.

Then he started telling about himself, "I work in a bank and I have three daughters, two are married and one has recently gone abroad along with her husband and my second daughter recently got married. She works with Infosys."

"That's great." I replied.

"My second daughter has gone downstairs and will be coming in a while. The youngest is Aastha" and pointed towards her. "Let's see, we need to find a suitable match for her." He said.

She was feeling shy at the time and probably thinking about me, I too was thinking about her. What is the necessity to find a suitable match for her when I am already there.

In between her sister came, Aastha introduced to her sister. We both exchanged greetings with each other.

"Oh, you are Ajay. I have heard quite a lot about you." Akshata (her sister) said.

"What have you heard about me.?" I said.

"Aastha mostly talks about you that you are talented and you are working and studying together." Akshata said.

"I too have heard a lot about you." I said.

"What have you heard?" Akshata asked.

"What you want to hear? The good or the bad ones." I said.

It was a humorous atmosphere and everyone was smiling after hearing this.

"You have a good sense of humor, how is your job going on?" Akshata asked.

"It's going good." I replied.

"On which technology do you work?" Akshata asked.

"I am working as a web developer." I said.

"Okay... that is cool." Akshata replied.

"On which technology, are you working?" I asked.

"I am working as Business analyst as well as Oracle DB." Akshata said.

"Great, since when are you working with Infosys and what is your current package?" I asked.

"I am working from the past 2 years and my current package is 3.5 lack pa."Akshata said.

"Oh, your package is too less. I guess." I said.

"I know, I am trying to switch company currently but there are very few openings and I am not able to crack any interview currently." Akshata said.

"Don't worry, you will indeed get a better package as you are a genius." I said.

"Please do not pull my leg, I am quite serious about this." Akshata said.

"I am sorry. Please send your resume to me, I will upload your resume on the referral portal and from there on you will definitely get soon." I said.

"Wow... That's great. Please share your email id. I will forward my resume to you." Akshata said.

"I will text you my email id on your number." I replied.

"Ok sure." Akshata said.

As we were involved in a deep conversation we didn't realize the time. It was already too late around 10.30pm. Aastha has served me the delicacies which are made especially during Diwali. Looking at the wall clock.

I said to Aastha's dad "Okay uncle, I am leaving as it's already too late. It's nice meeting you."

Aastha told me "Who will finish all this stuff."

"I had enough already" I replied.

On which Aastha in a dominating voice said, "You have to finish all this."

I smiled and said "Please let it be, I had enough." Uncle too said that very less is remaining so you do finish it off.

"Since I was eating all the time since morning I had enough sweets. So please let it be." I said.

"Okay. It's absolutely fine, whenever you feel home sick don't hesitate to come here." Uncle said.

I smiled and said "Sure. Thank You"

Aastha said to her family, she will see me off till parking and come back. We both reached the parking slot and she said lets stroll a little bit to which I agreed. We both were having a brisk walk near her home.

I held her hand to which she said "What are you doing? Everyone is watching us. Please do not indulge in such things as everyone knows me here. "

"It's okay. Let it be, anyways we are going to be a couple very soon." I said.

She smiled and said "Yes."

"How are you feeling, when I came to your home," I asked.

"I am speechless, at the same time feeling very happy that you met with my family. I hope to see you as part of my family very soon." She said.

"It's just what I am thinking too" I said.

"With every breath I feel you and also only your name is there in each and every breath of mine. I really like you from the bottom of my heart, if I don't speak to you even for a day I feel weird and something missing. To be honest, I love you from my heart, brain and body. "She said.

I smiled and said "Same here. I too can't leave without you even for a second. I can never imagine living without you. It really scares me when I think about it."

"Meri har sanso me tum hi ho…sirf tum hi ho,

Tumahri har sanso se chalti hai meri jindgi,

Ab to tum hi mere sab kuch ho,

Jina bhi tere sang aur marna bhi tere sang."

We both became very emotional. It was such a moment that we both could only understand. Finally she was getting too late. I took my bike and left.

As I was leaving, she told me to drive safely and message her as soon as I reach.

I said "Okay."

Last semester exam

As usual, one month before the semester's exam I didn't know this syllabus as well as the subject. There was a what's App group of our class on which I posted "Can anyone please send me, the syllabus and subject of this semester, also if anyone of you have any notes please do send me on my email id."

Some members of this group sent me the subject name of this semester

ISS

IP

DW

ST

OOSE

I was confused on reading this and replied, "buddy please send me the full form of these subjects, as I am unable to identify full name from their abbreviations."

Soon some of them pinged the full form of all the subjects.

ISS - "Information system security"

IP - "Internet programming"

DW - "Data warehousing"

ST - "Software Testing"

OOSE – "Object oriented software engineering"

I was looking at the subject names, I found that some subjects were easy and the rest I haven't heard about them earlier.

The examination schedule has arrived. They are starting from 12th November. I immediately called Aastha and asked her for all the notes of all subjects.

"Finally, you woke up from your sleep and realize that exams are round the corner." She said.

"Please let it be and please mail me all the subjects notes that you have." I said.

"Okay will be mailing you in a while." She said.

After some time I received all the notes. I was reading them and I found that some subjects were a bit too hard and really I needed to work hard on them.

I thought for a while how to get 60% marks, as anyways just passing usually easy and soon I started calculating how to achieve 60% marks for this semester.

My assumption is as follows:-

Subject	External		Internal	Total
IIS	35	+	15	50
IP	40	+	15	55
OOSE	35	+	15	50
DW	40	+	15	55
ST	40	+	15	55
Practical				80

345/ 6 = 57.5

Usually in practical's we get 90 out of 100 but my aggregate was coming down to 57 %. I realized that I need to work hard little bit harder for this semester. I started planning for all these subjects as usual, we always plan but never implement itand neither do we follow it. We always study at the eleventh hour and burn the midnight oil.

Around 10pm that same day I received a message from Aastha "I want to talk something important urgently."

"Yes Jaan, Say." I replied.

"I can't tell you on message. We need to meet and talk about this." She said.

"I need to know this right now." I replied.

"Can't you understand, I told you once that we need to meet and talk about this as I cannot message you?" She said.

I was confused. Why she is getting angry as I did nothing. "Okay, let it be. I don't want to know about this at all.. Good night." I replied.

After some time, she again messaged me "Sorry Jaan. I was a bit angry at that time."

I didn't reply. She again messaged me "Jaan, I am feeling lonely please do reply."

I was not in the mood to reply but as she said "Lonely"

I couldn't stop myself and replied "What happened? What you want to share with me."

"Jaan let it be. Let's talk something else." She said.

"No I want to know right now." I asked.

She agreed and said "Tomorrow some members of the groom's family are coming to see me."

"What?? How come all of a sudden? You should let everyone know in your family about our relationship, also do let them know that you are not ready for this marriage." I said.

I was very tensed and was making plans how to break up this marriage and I kept telling her that please don't worry as tomorrow they are just coming to see you nothing is finalized yet. As afterwards you can say that you didn't like the boy.

She simply replied "Yes."

I was very much worried and was trying to hold myself and deal with the current situation but was unable to think, how to make her understand as I was the one with whom she used to share all her personal feelings.

I was constantly telling her to stay calm and do not worry and told her "I will be coming to meet you tomorrow so as of now you just go to sleep."

In such a situation how can anyone sleep?

We both stopped sharing messages with each other but I was still confused. I was lying on the bed and my eyes were closed but my mind was still fighting with thoughts as what is going to happen. That night I couldn't sleep and neither did she.

Next Day early morning,

Usually I never woke up early morning. It was around 5 in the morning and I was thinking when it would be 9am so that I can call her, time is passing really slow. I was eagerly waiting for 9 o'clock. At last it is 9 in the morning and I called her but she was not receiving my calls.

I was much more tensed and told myself, "What the hell is happening? Why isn't she receiving my calls?"

It was time to go to the office but I was unable to think what to do. Should I go to the office? Or should I go to meet her? But without any reason I can't go directly to her home.

I decided to go to the office. After reaching office, I again called her but she did not receive my call again and this went on for more than 30 times.

That whole day I was in a lot of tension, around 7pm I received a message from her "What are you doing Jaan?"

I was very angry and upset with her and replied her "Can't you understand, I have been trying to call you since morning and you are not receiving my calls even I messaged you more than 100 times but you didn't reply."

"I already told you that today some members of the groom family are coming to see me so how do you expect to receive your call in between them." She replied in a harsh way.

"At least you could have replied to my message. You can't imagine through which phase I was going through the whole day." I said.

"I couldn't understand you." She said.

Really, it was a tough time for me to cope up with it everything was going against me. I was thinking through which phase of my life I was going through.

That day I was not feeling sleepy and unable to concentrate on anything. Also exams were going to start from next week. I wanted to study but in such a situation, how could anyone study.

It was one of the toughest times of my life. It was impacting on my performance in the office.

Finally exams started. I messaged her on the first day of our exam that I want to meet her to which she replied that I should study for the exam first as we can talk about this later on.

Really, I was confused and clueless as what to do? In such a situation, How could I focus on my studies as it was an important moment of my life.

Finally, it was the first day of exam.

It was IIS paper. I have no idea what to write for this paper. It was 10 o'clock in the morning. I received the question paper and after seeing this, I realized that I am unable to answer any question.

I was feeling like submitting the blank answer sheet and just walk off, as next semester I can clear this paper. Unfortunately, there was a rule during exam that we cannot leave the exam hall before one hour of the exam.

My roll no was 505 and behind me Sumeet was constantly poking me and saying to show him my answer sheet. I repeatedly told him that I haven't written anything but he was not willing to listen. I was quite angry and said, "Look what I have written?"

He was quite surprised at this as usually I never do this.

"Brother please writes something." He said.

"I am not in a mood to write anything." I replied to Sumeet

"I understand that you can leave this subject for next semester but just think about me, if I am unable to clear this subject I will be year down. Please do write something and share with me." Sumeet said.

"Okay, wait." I replied.

I was not in a mood to write anything but as there goes a famous proverb *"A friend in need is a friend indeed."* I started writing something.

I finally started to concentrate and started attempting the questions. As I started writing I kept on writing. Finally, our first paper was over.

At the end of the exam Sumeet said "Thanks a lot for helping me, hope I will clear this subject and also please continue helping me with the remaining subjects."

For the second exam, I was quite prepared and also found the questions really easy and I was able to attempt all the questions very easily.

After exam one of my friends told me that Madam was calling me. I went to meet madam near her cabin, I saw that Aastha was already seating with her.

"What have you both decided please let me know?" Madam said.

"Which decision are you talking about?" I asked.

"I want to know about your relationship as her would be husband is our principal's relative. Principal Sir saw you together many times. He told me to ask both of you as what is going on between them? " Ma'am said

"What should I tell him? That's why I wanted to talk to you." She said again.

"I am willing to marry Aastha and she knows everything about me and also about my decision." I replied.

She asked Aastha about her decision to which she replied "I cannot go against my parents."

Which indirectly means, she was not going to take this forward? After hearing this I couldn't hold myself and my eyes were fielded with tears. Ikept repeating things in my mind like "*I can't believe this is happening to me*" and asking It just didn't seem real, and I wondered when I would wake up from this horrible nightmare. *"Are you sure?"*

Ma'am again asked her "Don't take your decision in such a haste. I don't know how much serious you both are, you still have time till the last paper so think about it and let me know."

Looking at my face, ma'am could easily find out how serious I was. She asked me "What is your opinion about her decision?"

"What should I say, I really love her and also can't live without her. But ultimately it is her life so I will be happy with whatever decision she takes." I said.

"Yeah, I can find it from your face. How happy you were? As of now leave it, please concentrate for the next paper." Ma'am replied.

I too was surprised by her decision as this was the first time she said without any hesitation about her final decision.

I was feeling very depressed and lonely. After reaching home I started crying. I could not come out of this though. However hard I try I could not overcome it. I heard in such a situation wine becomes a good friend.

I made up mind to go and have a drink for a second but suddenly I realized that my roommates would really shout at me for such an act.

At 5 o'clock in the evening all my roommates came and they were shocked to see me that I was sitting very silently in one of the corner of our room. They were asking me something and I was not speaking to them.

My roommate Rajwent to the washroom and brought a bucket full of water and poured on me suddenly, all of a sudden I came back to sense and I got angry and I tightly slapped him on his face.

Raj did not feel bad about this, he gave his other cheek and said, "Common bro slap on this too."

They reminded me that they always told me that she was just making use of me and that I never listened.

"Now see, she didn't think about this at least once before taking this extreme decision for whom you were ready to die for. I always kept telling you that all girls are same." Raj said.

 I instantly reply no, "She is not one of them."

"I don't think so, she is just like any other girl, by the way you have your exam tomorrow so just prepare for it. Why are you spoiling your career because of her. "Raj said.

Raj further said "look another girl will definitely come into your life, but time will never come back so at this moment please concentrate on your studies."

The next day, I managed and wrote my exam but was not much confident about the answers that I wrote. I was now very much confident about her decision.

After our last exam I hurriedly came back to my home, all of my friends were calling me but I was not in a mood to meet anyone as I wanted to stay alone.

I was sitting alone. I blocked her from all my contact list i.e. Facebook, What's app etc.

After two days of our exam I received a message from her, from a different number stating that she wants to meet me. I replied back to her "Why do you want to meet me? As there is nothing left between us. "

"Please, I can't live without you, I just want to meet you and spend time with you." She said

After some time I said "Okay, tomorrow 10:30 am at my home."

"Okay, thanks." She replied.

It's your decision

It was the first time she came on time but I was not waiting for her. She was seated on the couch and she pulled my hand and made me sit along with her. I sat beside her. There was silence in the room and none of us was taking the initiative to speak up first. After some times she told me "Say something."

"There is nothing left to speak now. What should I say then? Whatever you wanted to say, already you have said that before, what is left now? It was completely your decision." I said.

"My dear, where am I going to leave you in between, I am always there by your side, trust me." She said.

I was totally shocked after hearing this as how suddenly she changed her decision, how did she make a turn over completely.

"Are you pulling my legs as I can't believe this, are you serious?"

"I am indeed serious, trust me." She said.

I was really fascinated after hearing this and was in a joyous mood. I was very happy but at the same time was speechless all I could do was hug her tightly. She kissed me and asked me, "Did you eat something?"

"No." I said.

"Alright, we will go out and eat something." She said.

"First of all as you have come to meet after a very long time and in that if you go outside so we will have really very less time to spend together. I want to spend some quality time with you alone together." I said.

"Alright, where will we eat then?" She said.

"I will do one thing, give me some time I will go downstairs. There is a hotel besides of fast food." I said. "I will parcel it and bring it here."

I came after sometime along with the parcel and we ate together. While eating, I told her, "Your sister called me in the morning."

"Why?" She asked.

"Her interview has been scheduled in my company. She was asking me what to study. She seemed a bit nervous while speaking. I guided her about what to study and prepare well for the interview." I said.

"That's good, it seems that you have befriended with my sister very well." Aastha said.

"For your sake I have to do this, anyhow once she joins my company then you too can say that at your home about this." I said.

"That's true." She said.

"After marriage where we will stay together?" I asked.

"What?" She asked.

"I mean, do we need to settle in Pune only or else in some other city like Bangalore, which is also a very good city to live in." I said.

"I think we will have to settle down in Pune itself as my parents will be left alone otherwise." She said.

"Alright, then we will try to find some accommodation nearby your home so that you can go easily to your parents' house whenever you want." I said.

"Yeah, It will be good." She said.

"When are you going to tell at your home about our relationship?" I asked.

"That's what I am thinking about as how and when should I talk to them." She said.

"I think once I secure a good job, then I too will gain some confidence within, so that I too will have a valid point to discuss with them." She said.

"Okay. Very well." I said.

"The boy who has come to see you. What do you know about him?" I asked.

"His name is Rachit. He works as Quality analyst in one of the IT firms and his package is around 4 to 5 lac." She said.

"I think I should directly talk to him and tell him about everything about our relationship so that he can understand it and most probably he will cancel this marriage from his side." Or you should talk to your parents and try to convince them and make them ready as well as they should accept about our relation, but be cautious before speaking up." I said.

"What do you think about this, will this work out?" I asked her.

"Let me think about it. You need not worry about this at all as when the time comes I will say everything to my parents and everything will be sorted out." She said.

"Okay." I said.

"We will make a routine from today onwards." I said.

"About what?" She asked.

"You want to work right? For that you need to work a little bit harder in order to secure a decent job. I am damn sure that whatever I taught you during last semester, you must have forgotten by now." I Said.

"Well, you are passing sarcastic comments regarding me? I haven't forgotten anything whatever you thought me last semester. I Just need to revise little bit." She said.

"Okay, at least you will have to revise along with me, agreed? As you know there are very few openings for fresher and in that too they ask a lot of things." I said.

"Very well Sir" She nodded her head.

That day I was very happy. I think that was one of the best days of my life. I was now confident that Aastha will convince her parent's anyhow. I thought that soon I will tell her that we should get engaged so that I will not have to bother about losing her again.This was all going around in my mind; I think I was totally lost in my own world.

Aastha asked me "Where have you lost, are you Alright?" I didn't utter a single word to her and just nodded my head.

"When are you going to say this in your home?" I asked.

"Let the proper time come." She said.

"Alright, but whenever you need my help do not hesitate to tell me as I will be readily available to help you." I said.

She smiled and said "Yes."

That same day around 8pm, I received a message from Aastha's sister.

"Hi Ajay. What's up?" Akshata asked.

"I am good, Thanks. What about you?" I said and asked.

"I am good too. I need to ask you something." Akshata replied.

"Yes, please." I said.

I have heard a couple of times from Aastha that Akshatais quite selfish and you should be very cautious about her. But I needed to come close to her for Aastha so that whenever Aastha says about our relationship to her parents that time Akshata should be by her side and should not oppose her. That's why I started to talk to her very seriously.

"You know what, I got a call from your company regarding the opening and they have scheduled an interview for me." Akshata said.

"That's great." I said.

"Please help me out. As what all they will ask." Akshata asked

"Mostly first round will be telephonic so in that they will probably ask about your profile, experience and maybe about your previous project. That's all I suppose they should ask during this round." I said.

"Okay, I am a bit nervous and tomorrow they have scheduled a telephonic round." Akshata said.

"Nervous and you? I have heard a lot about you and also you are a genius." I said.

"Shut up. As I am nervous and in such a time you are trying to pull my leg." Akshata said.

"Okay, don't worry. Let me help you out with how to speak. For that let me call you up." I said.

"Okay call me." Akshata said.

I called her and started explaining her, how to face the interview confidently. After this chat with her I thought that she gained some confidence as how to face tomorrow's telephonic interview.

Next day,

I was in office it was around 11o'clock and I was busy with my work. At that time I received call from Akshata "I asked her what happened?"

"It's already 11am, still didn't receive the call for the interview as it was scheduled for the same time." She said.

I told her "Sometimes it happens as the technical panel may be busy with some other candidates for the interview. Please wait for your turn they will definitely call you."

"Alright." She said.

Then I continued with my work. After some time she massaged "Interview was quite good." I replied "That's good. Let me check the status of your interview and then will get back to you."

"Okay, thanks." She said.

Almost get close

After two days,

Akshata called me in the morning. I was getting ready to leave for office. I was quite surprised as usually she doesn't call me at this time, I was scared as if Aastha has said anything to Akshata about our relationship. I gathered some confidence and receive the call and said in a very low tone, "Hello Akshata."

"Hello Ajay." She replied

"How come you called me such early morning, Is everything alright?" I asked.

"Did you check?" Akshata said.

I was totally blank as what she was asking for because I was still in a fantasy world with Aastha.

"What I was supposed to check?" I asked.

"Oyeedamboo, it's already passed two days, still I didn't receive any update regarding my interview result." She said.

"Be calm, don't worry. You will receive soon, currently I am leaving for office will check on the portal and let you know." I replied.

"Alright." She said.

As soon as I reached the office, I opened a referral drive portal to check the interview status of Akshata. I observed that her status was not yet updated. I messaged Akshata that her status is under process.

I told her, "don't worry as soon as I receive any updates regarding this, I will let you know."

"Thanks a lot." She said.

I was still thinking too, why her status was not updated on the portal. I guess, I was more serious than Akshata regarding her interview result status. Every single hour I was checking the portal to check her status.

It was around 3pm and till now her status was not yet updated I thought that maybe her status will not change for today. I decided to close the portal and not to open for today because of this I was not able to concentrate on my work.

As I was about to close the portal I notice that her status has changed. After seeing her status I couldn't control myself as I was very happy.

I took my phone and went to the conference room to call her, but she was not reachable. I tried a couple of times and finally it was reachable.

As soon as she received the call I said, "Congratulations..!! I want a party."

"For what reason?" She asked.

"You are selectedhere, Just now it got updated on the portal." I said,

"Really, thanks Ajay. All credit goes to you." She replied.

"What did I do? It was your hard work which paid off. Now leave this thing. When are you giving me a party? "I said.

"You will definitely get soon before that let me first receive an offer letter." She replied.

I thought how selfish she is, what trouble she might have if she could have said yes for the party. I was not serious about the party, was just trying to pull her leg.

"Be prepared for the HR round as it totally depends on how you handle it." I said to her.

"Sure, Sorry Ajay will talk to you later as I think I am getting a call from your company." She replied.

"Alright and all the best." I replied.

I was very happy that she was finally selected and I could heave a sigh of relief. I messaged Aastha that your sister has been selected.

"That's great news. Thanks a lot for everything. Finally, you did it." She said.

"I had to do it for you." I replied.

That same day in the evening I messaged Akshata "What are you doing?"

"Nothing just came from the office and watching movie." She replied.

I was thinking to ask her what she thinks about me and Aastha's relationship. I wanted to know her opinion.

"Hi, I need your help." I replied.

"What type of help?" She replied.

"Promise me that you will help me for sure. " I asked.

"First tell me then will decide." She said.

I thought this was the perfect time to know about her opinion.

"You know what, I am in love with a girl even she loves me." I said.

"That's cool, but what help do you want from me in this." She asked.

"What do you think. How can she tell her family about our relationship?" I asked.

"Really, I don't have any idea on this, can't help you. Also, I don't like love marriages. Kindly don't expect anything from my end." She said.

She didn't ask me even a single time about who was that girl.

"At least you should help me some time." I said.

"Sorry, I really can't help you on this. Don't expect anything from me on this." She replied.

"Chill, no worries. Will not ask you again." I said.

I tried to change the topic. I felt that she has become quite friendly with me but at the same time I also felt that she at no cost will help me on this. I realized that Aastha was right as her sister is really very selfish and cunning.

As days passed by, me and Akshata became very close friends and I started sharing my personal matters with her.

I decided to tell Akshata about my relationship, also the girl whom I was talking about was none other than Aastha (her sister), before that I called Aastha and said," I am telling everything to your sister."

"Regarding?" Aastha replied.

"About our Love" I said.

"No, you won't tell her anything." Aastha replied.

"Why should I not say? When are you going to say, after your marriage?" I said.

"Hmmmm" She said

"What? Hmm ..,I am about to say everything to Akshata." I said.

"For my sake, you won't say anything to her. If you really love me." She replied.

I was quite angry at this and in a rude voice I said," Really, I don't understand. What do you want? Whenever I ask you, you always tell me to keep quiet."

"Even I am not able to understand anything. You are right. You don't know me completely." She said.

"Alright, what you want to do? You do? Don't expect from me anything. Good bye." I said and disconnected the phone.

She didn't reply me either.

Engagement

It was more than five days, till now I didn't receive any message from her. I was missing her and was getting restless. Every moment I was thinking to call her and ask how is she.

At the same time I was not able to understand as to why she is not messaging me. I was totally clueless as what was happening. I too decided not to message her or call her.

It was Friday I was returning home from office cab. I messaged Shreya, "Hi, how are you?"

She replied, "I am fine what about you?"

Shreya was my former colleague. She was cute, adorable. We used to share our lunch in my previous company.

"What to tell you now? I am in bit tension. I am not able to understand anything." I said to Shreya.

"Why? What happened?" She asked.

I told everything to her about my love story and said please help me in this.

"Don't think about this too much. What is going to happen will happen also she has already said no to you once. I think you should tell everything to her sisterand then see how they react to this." Shreya said to me.

"If I tell everything to her sister than she could land in big trouble from her family." I said,

"Look here, I also did love marriage so I know better than you. This is not the right way as what she likes she will do. She should consult with you about each and everything. After hearing your story I think that she is making a fool of you. Don't think too much about this and tell everything to her sister, so that afterwords you won't repent that you didn't say anything to her sister. No one knows what is written in destiny." Shreya said.

 I was totally convinced after talking to Shreya and made my mind to tell everything to Akshata.

I messaged her," Hi, I want to talk to you something urgent."

It has passed around 10 minutes but still I didn't receive any reply from her. I again messaged her but still didn't receive anything. I said to myself, "What the hell is going on. Why isn't she is replying to my message."

I cursed her in my mind. "She is too selfish, she never responds timely." I was continuously checking my mobile whether I received any message from her. For the last time I messaged her, "Once you are free. Please message me."

Next day in the morning around 8 o'clock, I received a message from Akshata, "Hi Ajay, Sorry I was quite busy yesterday. What happened?" I thought that I should tell everything to her but before telling, I just asked her casually, "If it's my work. You will be busy every time, anyways where were you busy?"

She replied, "Yesterday was Aastha's engagement ceremony, Was busy in that." As soon as I read this, I was completely taken aback. I was not able to think anything. What should I do now.

The pain engulfed me, and at times it seemed never-ending. I felt like I was literally buried, eye-ball-deep in sadness.

I felt robbed of the beautiful future that I thought we would have together. We had just moved into the type of home that you start a family in.

I felt so hurt that he could just transfer his affections to someone else, literally overnight, and seemingly without batting an eyelash. I was amazed at how hard this hit me.

"You were going to tell me, which was something urgent." She messaged me again.

"As usual, I messaged you." I replied.

"Are you sure?" She asked.

"Yes, bye for now. Getting late for office, will talk to you later." I said.

"Really?" She asked.

I didn't reply after that message.

Immediately I messaged Aastha, "Congratulations…!!!"

"I am sorry." She replied.

"Good bye forever. I have never seen such a deceiver like you before." I said.

"I want to meet you." She replied.

"Now what is left between us? I don't want to meet such liar like you." I said.

"For my sake, you will have to meet me." She replied.

"It's off no use meeting you now." I said.

"For our love, you will have to come." She replied.

"What love? Should I tell you something? Now I understand the true meaning of love, and all credit goes to you for helping me understand this."

After that I didn't reply her messages. Next day in the morning,

I was getting calls from Aastha, I was in no mood to talk to her. I was a bit confused whether I should receive her call and more important than that, why was she calling me at this time. I didn't receive her call but I couldn't hold myself from going apart from her.

I was not receiving her call "I am waiting for you in the parking of your home." She messaged me.

"I am not at home. I am in the office." I replied.

"I know, you are telling lies to me. You are at home only. Since when you started going to the office so early." She asked.

"I was having some urgent work in office so had to leave early." I replied.

"How much more will you lie. I can see your vehicle in the parking." She said.

"I have gone to office by Cab." I said.

"I am damn sure. You are at home only. Till you don't come I will wait for you here only." She replied.

"As you like. You do whatever." I said in a harsh way.

At the same time, I was not able to hold myself from staying away from her. My mind was stopping me to go and meet her but my heart was still telling me to meet her. Finally, I decided to meet her and went down.

When I saw her, I couldn't hold myself. I ran towards her, she was also excited. As soon as I reached near her, I saw Mehdi on her hand as well as the engagement ring. After looking at all this stuff, I was totally broke from inside, but I tried to smile and hold myself.

"Many many congratulations. All the best for your future." I said.

As soon as I said this, I could see tears in her eyes. She could not say anything to me. She held my hand, gathered some courage and said, "I am extremely sorry. What to do Jaan..! Everything happened in front of me, but I couldn't do anything."

I freed my hand from her and said, "I trusted you a lot but you have betrayed me. You have broken my heart. "You know what, you didn't want to say anything about our relationship at your home. The truth is that, you never ever loved me."

"It is certainly not like that, you will never understand." She replied.

"Yes, I do not want to understand now, you taught me everything by this." I said.

"Jaan, I love you. I am totally yours. Who has said that by living together only love blossoms? I will pray to god that if I have rebirth again, then I will be yours." She said.

"Stop this drama of yours, enough of that, you are talking about meeting in our next life? What about this life? You have betrayed me in this life, then how can I trust you for the next life."

What I wanted to understand. I understood. There is nothing more to understand. What you wanted to do, you did. I don't expect anything further from you.

The fact is that, I really loved you from the bottom of my heart and blindly trusted you as well, but you broke my heart and played with my emotions. If god is there, then he will definitely give justice?

It was love for me, but lust for you. I was totally wrong; I think I was a fool, who wanted to make someone mine.

In the choked voice she said, "Jaan don't say like this."

What should I say then, If you really love me, still there is time left as you are currently just engaged not married.

"How can I say this at my home as now the groom's family is too involved in this, also everyone in my family is happy with this. As well as my fiancé has done MBA and comes from a wealthy background." She said.

"Oh my god! Now I understood that you love money instead of a person. Should I tell you something, now do not say anything in your home. When my well-wishers told me about this, I didn't trust them, but finally after hearing from you. I realize this that they were right.

"What all are you thinking about, this is completely baseless how can I make you understand." She said.

"I don't want to hear anything further, in fact I think I am thinking in the right way now." I said.

One thing I will tell you, *"If it's not forever, it's not love"*

I know that, you won't say anything to anyone but remember one thing I am always there by your side and also I will wait for you. From your decision, I have come to know everything that "It was not love rather it was lust"

One drunken night with hopes

It was almost all over, I never thought in my wildest dreams that she would ever do like this to me. I was totally lost in my own world and was unaware as what I was doing and next what I was up to.

I used to blindly trust her, she broke my trust completely. How could she do this to me? I was thinking about her all the time and the most important thing was all my roommates had gone to their home town. I was completely alone with no one to talk to.

My whole routine was disturbed, no proper time to eat, when should I go to office, everything was disturbed. It was indeed very testing time for me.

I think that, I was not going to the office from the past 5 days also, I had purposefully switched off my mobile as I was not in a mood to talk to anyone.

It was Saturday morning around 9.30. My door bell was continuously ringing, I thought that I was dreaming it. But continuously someone was ringing the bell, hurriedly I woke up and saw that the doorbell was actually ringing.

I rushed towards the door and opened and was quite surprised to see that Suman my office colleague standing at the door and I thought Suman would be surprised too after seeing me in such a condition.

I was looking quite shabby also I haven't shaved from quite a few days. He was completely set aback after seeing me and was thinking what has happened to me.

He asked me "What happened to you? Why are you not coming to office, is everything Alright? Everyone was worried about you in the office as why are you not coming to office. We also tried to contact you on your mobile phone, but it was continuously switched off. Because of this behavior of yours, they were thinking of releasing you from the project.

They asked me about you. I told them that he is unwell because of this he is unable to come to office."

I was just listening to Suman but could not tell anything.

What have you made yourself, did you look yourself in the mirror. I could see drastic makeover between previous Ajay and current one.

Look my brother; you are quite smart and sensible than me. I would like to tell you one thing, as you know that we both are very close friends and mostly we used to share personal matters with each other.

I understand what happened is really very sad and forget all this is also difficult, but the more you think about this the more you will hurt yourself by recollecting your old memories. Life doesn't stop for anyone, you need to keep moving ahead. In such a young age, you have achieved a good designation.

You are smart and handsome. You will get a much better girl than her. So chill, enjoy new phase of life.

The most important thing you didn't betray her. So don't be upset with your life and remember one thing, don't do such thing in life that will hurt someone.

He was continuously saying and I was simply listening to him. In between He was asking me are you understanding what I am trying to tell you or not?

"Yes" I said.

Now do one thing go to the saloon and change your look I want the previous Ajay's look, also you have made a mess of your room.

You get ready by the time I will watch TV also we will make a plan for the evening.

"Okay" I said.

He called all the friends to discuss the plan for the evening.

I was ready and when He saw me. He said, "Trust me, you are looking very handsome and I think you are back to your original look."

He took out his mobile from his pocket. It was having a 13 mega pixel camera and said "Look here and smile please."

He took a picture of mine and posted it on Facebook and soon people started liking my new picture also commented on it as well.

"Can you see how much people like your new picture, now this is your true value, you thoroughly deserved this, and see you were willing to end your life just for the sake of a girl. Try to understand your inner abilities." Suman said.

"Enough for the day, I understood everything whatever you said. Thanks a lot for your advice." I replied.

He smiled and said "Alright, by the way, what different pattern of shirts you have."

"Why?" I asked.

"We are planning tonight to go to a night club." Suman said.

"I am in no mood to go anywhere." I said.

"At least you can give it a try, come along with me, I promise you won't feel bored, trust me you will feel as if you are in heaven. You haven't seen the whole world that's why you are in such a depression. I am not going to hear anything, you are going to come with me."Suman said.

It was around 9pm, we reached Marriott hotel in Pune. This is a famous nightclub. We entered inside the nightclub and straight away went to the dance floor. It was on the 8th floor.

There was a bouncer standing near the entrance to whom we showed our entry pass and he put stamp on our hand as a confirmation of entry pass.

As soon as we went inside, the music was being played at very high volume and we couldn't resist ourselves from dancing.

There were already a lot of people dancing and we too joined them. Suman came near me and whispered in my ear, "Look here, my brother how many hot girls are here. You can see all round here. Let's try to catch with them."

There were really many hot girls all around, I couldn't stop myself from watching them.

Suddenly, a very hot and sexy girl came in front of me and said, "Hey, wanna dance with me?"

After hearing this, I was quite surprised and was a bit shy to join her on the dance floor. I just smiled and said, "I am in no mood to dance as of now, you can go ahead."

She forced me to come along with her. Finally I agreed and joined her. While dancing, she asked me, "Will you have a drink along with me?"

As this was my first time, how could I say that I do not drink, and on top of that she was forcing me to have drinks.

"What will you have?" She asked

"Lime juice." I said.

"You must be joking" She said.

I smiled and asked "What are you having in drinks?"

"I will definitely go for Vodka." She said.

I was totally confused, what to have as I even didn't know the brand names of beer. I started thinking a lot and suddenly something clicked me and said "I will go for Rum."

She was quite amused after hearing this and said, "Are you sure? As rum is quite hard and one gets inebriated, very quickly."

I have made up my mind that I am going to have drinks anyhow. I said to her, "Definitely."

The bartender asked us "How much do you want?"

"Give us one pack." She replied.

It was my first time. I was feeling a little bit awkward. We cheered our drinks and started drinking. We again hit the dance floor. I was totally in an inebriated condition after some time. I asked her, "Can we have another peg."

"I don't think that you should have as already you have taken a lot." She said.

"This is nothing, this is just a beginning. I am very habitual to this." I replied.

She had no idea about me so she kept mum. We had another round of peg. I don't really remember what happened after that.

Next day in the morning,

When I woke up, I was lying on my bed. I was shocked as when I came back home and what really happened last night. I hurriedly got up from my bed and came in the drawing room and saw Suman sleeping on the sofa.

I woke him from his sleep. He asked "What happened?"

"When did we come back home last night as I really don't remember anything." I asked.

"I will let you know everything afterword as of now let me sleep." Suman said.

I was very curious to know, what exactly happened last night. I was constantly pushing him to get up.

"Do one thing, take my mobile, there is a video in it. Just watch it. You will come to know, what happened. " Suman said.

"Where is your mobile?" I asked.

It's on your computer table. I went inside and took the mobile and played the video, which he has recorded. It was around 30 minute video. I was totally shocked after seeing it. As this video was of me fully drunk.

I saw in the video that, I was constantly telling Suman that please take me to Aastha's home, so that I can say to her family about our relationship. How can she do like this to me.

She is involved in double standard as sometimes. She loves me and when not in a mood she starts hating me. What the hell she thinks about her? This is my heart, not any hospice that whenever she feels like coming she will come and then will walk away.

Suman was telling me, Due to some reason she would have said "No."

What could be the reason? When did I say to her that we will run away and get married? I was just saying that you should talk to your parent's at least once.

If her parents say no then I am alright with it. Our paths will never meet again if it was no from their end. She was so selfish that neither did she said anything to her parent's about this nor did she allowed me to do so.

What does she think about herself, if she can do like this then I am not going to leave her. Take me to her home right now. I will settle the matter today itself. Let us come to a conclusion in front of everyone.

"Will you listen to me it's too late to go to her home. We will go to her home tomorrow morning for sure, I myself will accompany you." Suman was saying to me.

"What late are you talking about? Alright, you don't take me along with you. I have another option with me. I will send photos of us to her fiancé then I will see how can this marriage goes forward. If she can do such thing to me then I will also ensure that her marriage doesn't happen.

"Okay, my brother we will do whatever you said. Let's go home now. It's too late. We will look into this tomorrow morning." Suman said.

"Okay, you are my true friend. Remember one thing never ever love anyone too much. There is nothing like love, it's all bullshit all are selfish in this world. They behave according to their needs." I said.

"I will never love anyone." Suman said.

After watching this video, I was totally shocked and couldn't believe that it was me in this video. By that time Suman woke up and said to me, "Did you see now, how you came back home."

"I am thankful to you, to bring me safely home." I replied.

"Can I tell you one thing, the way in which you were talking yesterday, trust me I too felt like crying. I never expected that you love her so much. Really, I felt that she should talk to her parents at least once. If you say I can talk to her once." Suman said.

"Leave it, if she really cares about me. She could have at least messaged or called me." I said

"I can't believe that people are so selfish like this, let me massage her. " Suman said.

"Alright then do whatever you feel is good." I said

Last message

Suman was thinking to text Aastha from my mobile. He was asking for my mobile. I told him "if you really want to message her then do it from your mobile as she won't reply, if you message her from mine."

Suman agreed and messaged Aastha from his mobile. He wrote "Hi Aastha, this is Ajay's friend, Just want to talk to you about something urgent."

"What do you want to talk with me?" Aastha replied.

"Well, I really don't know much about your relationship, but one thing I would like to tell you that you are not doing good. Please think about it again, you don't know about Ajay's condition and through which phase of his life he is going through." Suman said.

"You don't advise me what is wrong and right. I am already engaged now, please try to make your friend understand about this. I can't do anything now. Everyone in my family is quite excited about this and I don't want to disappoint them." She replied.

"Are you really happy with all this?" Suman asked.

"Yes, I am and also telling your friend that my wedding has been fixed on 12th of June if he wants to come he can." She said.

"I can't believe this. Ajay was right, he told me that not to message you. Now I really understand why he was telling me like this. You are really very selfish." Suman replied.

I took Suman's phone read the text message conversation between Suman and Aastha. After reading, I had tears in my eyes. I replied.

"Teri yaadon ke sahare ji raha hoon

Agar tumhe meri yaad aaye to laut aana

Kuch waqt achchha guzaara hai sath tumhare

Wo waqt agar yaad aaye to laut aana..."

Tumhara Rat.

****